HOPE
everlasting

A story about the amazing
power of faith, hope and love

There is always
hope!

♡

[signature]

HOPE
everlasting

A story about the amazing
power of faith, hope and love

J. C. LAFLER

REDEMPTION
PRESS

Published by Redemption Press, PO Box 427, Enumclaw, WA 98022

Toll Free (844) 2REDEEM (273-3336)

Redemption Press is honored to present this title in partnership with the author. The views expressed or implied in this work are those of the author. Redemption Press provides our imprint seal representing design excellence, creative content, and high quality production.

ISBN: 978-1-68314-439-7 (Paperback)
978-1-68314-440-3 (Hard Cover)
978-1-68314-441-0 (ePub)
978-1-68314-442-7 (Mobi)

Library of Congress Catalog Card Number: 2017949442

For I know the thoughts that I think toward you, says
the Lord, thoughts of peace and not of evil, to give
you a future and a hope.

Jeremiah 29:11 NKJV

Dedication

In loving memory of my grandfather O. D. Hewitt and my sister Becky Jean Hewitt: They rest in heaven but are never forgotten.

Acknowledgments

With much appreciation to the owner and staff of Redemption Press: You are an amazing group of people, and I am so thankful to have you as my friends and publisher. You keep me writing and inspire me to always look to God first. Thank you!

Prologue

He was sitting on the dirty floor of the storage shed. It was cold, dark, and smelly. It was located just outside the kitchen, and there was a bag of rotting potatoes sitting in the corner. They wasted so much food, and yet they denied him the basics. Their dogs ate better than he did. The smell of the rotting potatoes made his empty stomach churn. His head pounded where it had hit the wall when the "man of the house" (as only he called himself) shoved him away after beating him with a belt for not ironing his shirt exactly the way he wanted. Of course, it was never right, no matter how he did it. He knew it never would be. It was simply an excuse for another beating.

His back and legs were burning with pain, and now he would miss another day of school and the chance for a little extra food. He knew he couldn't take much more of this abuse. They kept threatening to take him out of school for good, and he wouldn't wait for that to happen. The food he got at school was the only thing that kept him going. He was going to have to run again, and this time he would keep going until he got out of the state completely. It was the only thing left to ensure his survival.

A fuzzy picture of his mom flashed into his mind along with her constant reminder, "God is with us, and there is always hope." The last four years had taken their toll, and he was losing those memories and any form of hope. The picture in his mind slid away with his tears.

Chapter 1

After dropping off the baby at the home for girls, he wandered for hours. Dawn arrived, bathing the sky in early morning light. Eventually, he left the road to follow a path that seemed to go on forever—just two dirt tracks running through a field. He didn't have any money left for the bus, and everything he owned was in the backpack on his back. He was lost in both mind and spirit. He had nowhere to go and nobody who cared. At least the baby had a chance of finding someone who would love and care for her. That time had passed for him. His mother had died when he was ten, and part of him had died with her. His father was never in the picture, and his mom hadn't liked to talk about it. It had something to do with the war, and she always cried when he asked about it, so he had quit asking.

Four years of living in foster homes had produced nothing but fear and pain, but even those were over for him. He would turn sixteen at the end of the month. Two years of being a runaway and scrounging for food and shelter had aged him even more. Still, if he got in any trouble, or someone recognized him as a runaway, it would not be good for him. And if anyone found out about him leaving the baby, it would be bad, really bad. He still couldn't believe that Star had left her baby and walked away. It just proved, once more, that you really couldn't trust anyone.

After hours of walking, he saw an old barn up ahead. It looked like it had held hay and tools at one time, probably for working in the fields, maybe even for animals. The barn was old, weathered, and appeared to be deserted. It was obviously abandoned and had been left to fall apart, just like him. He made his way to the door hanging by one hinge and looked inside.

There was still some hay in the barn and a couple of old horse blankets hanging on large hooks in one wall.

On the other side of the doorway was a rickety ladder leading up to a loft of sorts. A couple of old burlap bags hanging over the edge suggested it had been used as a place to store seed or corn to keep it off the floor where it would stay dry. Tentatively checking each step of the ladder to make sure it would hold his weight, he climbed up. The loft was not as old as the rest of the building; the wood was newer. There were several wooden crates in the corner. He climbed carefully onto the platform, testing each step to make sure it was sturdy enough to hold his weight. It creaked a bit but felt solid as he walked across to look in the crates. The first couple of crates were empty, but one held old chains and tractor parts. There was a large tractor seat propped up behind them in the corner.

Once he determined the loft was sturdy, he had an idea. He grabbed a couple of the burlap bags and went back down the ladder where he had seen some hay. He stuffed the large bags full of the hay, and one by one, he carried them back up to the loft. He arranged the crates along the front edge of the platform and pulled the foam out of the cracked tractor seat. Going back for another trip, he took the remaining bags and filled them with hay. Again, he carted them up to the loft. He also pulled the heavy blankets from the hooks on the wall and carried each of them up to the loft. He was sweaty and exhausted, but he finally had all the bags and the blankets up on the loft platform. Arranging them tight together, he was able to make a rough mattress on the other side of the crates with the foam at the top. He placed one of the blankets over them and lay down to try them out. It was bearable, and using the other blanket to pull over him, he had a place to sleep that was protected from view by the row of crates. It was warmer than being outside, and he needed to rest.

It was so quiet in the barn. A sort of peace settled over him. He was strained and anxious from the past couple of days and tired from the hours of walking. It wasn't long before he drifted off to sleep. He dreamed about the girl and her baby.

They had met at the homeless shelter right after she had the baby. The baby didn't have a name because she said she couldn't keep her. She called herself Star, but he didn't think that was really her name.

Sometimes when he spoke to her, she didn't answer him; it was as if she didn't know he was talking to her. They were traveling from town to town, staying in old buildings when they could find one, and eating what they could get their hands on. He had sold his leather boots to get enough money for formula, diapers, and fast food burgers, never expecting her to take off and leave him with the baby. Now all he had left were worn-out sneakers he had picked up at the homeless shelter along with a ragged coat, hat, and thin gloves they had provided. He had left the only blanket he had with the baby, so he would have to find another. He needed a job where someone would give him a chance. He had no references and no way to dress for an interview, so as soon as an employer got a good look at him, they dismissed him.

In his dream, the girl was talking sweetly to the baby, holding her close and making her smile. Then the girl turned into his mom, and she was telling the baby she loved him. *Him?* Was he the baby? He tossed and turned on the uncomfortable bed and finally fell into a deeper sleep.

Chapter 2

He was born Jeremiah David Stewart, but his mom always called him Miah. He hated when foster parents and other kids shortened his name to Jerry, so he had been telling people his name was Miah since he had been on his own. It made him feel better to hear people refer to him by the name his mother used. He had left foster care almost two years before and vowed never to go back. It meant he had to leave everything behind and move to a different state, but it was worth getting away from some of the other situations he had been involved in. He hadn't had good luck as a foster child; they had treated him as everything from a servant, babysitter, and housecleaner, to a scapegoat and punching bag. Other than a couple of sympathetic teachers and foster care workers, no one even saw him as a real person any more.

When he finally gave up on having anything even resembling a family again, he hit the road. After spending days hiding in the trees and old buildings along the highway, he had hitched a ride with a truck driver and managed to get out of the state. He survived by using homeless shelters and finding odd jobs to earn money for food. He got extra clothing at the Salvation Army, and the lady running it felt sorry for him and provided leather boots and a backpack containing basic toiletries. He managed to find truck stops or churches where he could slip in and take an occasional hot shower, and he also learned to slip in among large groups holding picnics or cookouts in order to obtain food if he didn't have money. When he ran into Star at the homeless shelter a couple of months ago, he thought he had found a kindred spirit, and he felt good about trying to help her. But all that had gotten him was a faster end to the little bit of cash he had managed to scrape up and the anxiety of being left with an infant. At least he had found the baby a place to stay, and he hoped she would be treated a lot better than he had been since his mother died. As far as Star went, he feared for her future. Unfortunately, it had been taken out of his hands.

Miah shivered in his sleep and tried to pull the blanket closer around him. Still, the cold crept in and settled into his bones. Used to rough environments, he slept on, completely spent by all that had occurred in the past twenty-four hours.

In the morning, Miah woke stiff and cold. Making his way outside, he continued on the path that had led him to the barn. He needed food and water. There had to be someone close by who owned the barn. The path seemed endless, and he felt as dead at the fields around him. It was very cold, but the sun shone brightly, oblivious to the desolate landscape. Hours dragged by, before he spotted smoke up ahead coming from what looked like a chimney. He picked up the pace, hoping for at least something to drink. As he got closer, he could see an old farmhouse and a barn in much better shape than the one he left that morning. At least there were chickens in the yard and several cows in the field behind it. A meager pile of wood was stacked on the uneven porch at the front of the house. An axe rested on a log beside the porch next to several logs that had been dragged near it.

Hesitantly, Miah made his way up the steps of the porch, hoping that someone inside would at least give him a glass of water. He knocked on the door and could smell the wonderful scent of bacon and eggs as an elderly man opened the door just a crack to ask him what he wanted.

"Hello, sir," Miah said softly, "I wonder if you could spare a glass of water?"

The old man hesitated, asking Miah where he was from and why he needed water.

"I have been traveling looking for work," Miah said quickly. "Do you need a hand with getting the rest of that wood cut? I would be willing to work for meals and a place to stay for a couple of days."

Before the old man could respond, an elderly woman pushed open the door holding a glass of water. "Come in out of the cold for a moment," she said, opening the door wider and handing the glass of water to Miah as he came in. "What are you thinking?" she said to the man. "It's freezing outside."

Miah downed the water quickly, thankful for the woman's generosity. The smells coming from the kitchen made his stomach growl loudly, and the woman heard it. She took the empty glass from Miah and asked him if he'd had breakfast yet. When he shook his head no, she insisted he join them.

"Now Maggie," the man spoke quickly, "we don't know this boy at all."

"Well, I can see he is hungry, and I can hear his stomach growling, so I know he needs something to eat. Do you want to send him on his way without anything? He looks like a strong wind would blow him away!"

The man turned toward Miah and said sternly, "Can we trust you, young man?"

Chapter 3

Miah nodded quickly, thinking he would give just about anything for a hot meal in this warm house. He followed the man and the woman he had called Maggie into the kitchen. It was simple, but clean, with a wooden table and four chairs in the corner. Two plates and silverware were waiting, and Miah could see the bacon and eggs he had smelled earlier. Maggie told him to wash up at the sink as she added another plate and silverware to the table along with a tall glass of milk. The warm water felt good on his cold fingers, and Miah quickly added a squirt of soap he found next to the faucet. He dried his hands and joined the man and Maggie at the table, taking off his backpack and hanging it and his coat and hat on the back of the chair.

As he sat down, Maggie introduced the man as her husband, Odee. They then bowed their heads as Odee began to pray. Miah knew about praying from his mom, so he folded his hands and bowed his head. After the prayer, Maggie took her husband's plate and went back to the stove. She piled on eggs, bacon, and a thick slice of bread. Carrying the plate back to the table, she set it in front of Odee. She repeated the process with Miah's plate and finally her own.

They ate in silence for a few minutes, and Miah took his time. The food was delicious! He found himself enjoying hot scrambled eggs and crisp bacon along with homemade bread. He couldn't remember when he had last eaten anything so good!

Maggie watched the young man and wondered what his story and background was. He was obviously hungry and painstakingly thin. He looked like a sad, dirty teenager, and she wondered why he was alone. She knew Odee needed some help around the farm, but she wasn't sure this boy was the answer. Still, maybe they could give him a chance.

Odee also watched Miah as he slowly devoured every crumb of the breakfast. He was trying to judge whether this boy was worth investing time in. He wondered if the boy would even be helpful around the farm. He could really use a hand because the chores and upkeep of the farm were more than he could handle on his own. Their only son, Derric, had moved away this past summer after marrying a girl he met in college. Though he was happy for the newlyweds, it meant that he must handle the many chores around the farm. While Odee knew there was more work to do than he could handle on his own, he never told Derric that. He didn't want his son to worry. He remembered Pastor John talking about worrying and reminding everyone about God providing for your every need at last Sunday's service, and he wondered if this boy was a blessing from God or just another troubled teenager. Either way, he knew Maggie would probably expect him to give it a shot.

Miah was aware of the couple's watching eyes. He tried to use his best manners and eat the food slowly. He didn't know how long it would be before he found another meal. He wondered if he dared to ask them again about helping around the farm. Maybe he shouldn't press his luck, but he wasn't sure how far it was to the next town. He would, at least, have to ask them about that.

As Miah finished the wonderful meal, Odee put down his own silverware, wiped his mouth with his napkin, and spoke for the first time since he had finished praying. "You were asking about chopping the wood. Are you really looking for work?" He looked out the window and back at Miah. "Would you be willing to help with other chores as well . . . if we were interested in hiring you, that is?"

"Yes, sir," Miah replied quickly. "I can help with anything you want. For meals and a place to sleep, I would be willing to help you out for a while. I don't mind sleeping in the barn, either. Anything would be fine."

"Well, let's start with the wood today and see how it goes," Odee stated quietly. "We go through a lot of wood in the winter months, and I have not been able to keep up. Finish your breakfast and meet me outside. I will get you some work gloves and show you where I want the wood stacked." Odee got up from the table and headed outside.

"Don't mind him," Maggie commented. "Would you like more to eat?"

"No, mam," Miah replied. "It was very good! I better get outside and start chopping wood." Miah got up from the table and quickly put his ragged coat back on as Maggie took the last dishes over to the sink. He headed back outside. He didn't want to take a chance of blowing this job opportunity. He wanted to please Odee and make sure he could do enough to earn a warm place to sleep tonight and another meal. He was tired of running and never knowing what the day would bring, and he hated being alone at night in the dark.

Chapter 4

As he stepped out on the porch, Miah saw Odee come out of the barn and head in his direction. He gave him a pair of warm, sturdy work gloves and led him over to the side of the house where the fallen logs were lying. He showed him how to chop the logs into chunks then upright them and use a splitter to chop them into the right size. At first, Miah was hesitant swinging the ax, but before long, he found a rhythm to the whole process and had a small pile of wood ready to carry and stack. Odee showed him where and how much to stack on the porch and where to stack the excess at the side of the shed. He explained that he wanted to get a large surplus, which they would cover with canvas in case the weather kept them from chopping for any length of time.

As Miah worked, Maggie watched from the window. She wondered again what his story was and why he was alone and without a home. She had taken a quick peek in his backpack and knew the boy didn't have much to his name. She prayed he was a good boy and would please Odee. She knew her husband desperately needed help around the farm, so maybe God had sent them this boy after all. Maybe they could help each other.

Maggie went upstairs and looked into Derric's old bedroom. He had taken all the things he wanted when he left the farm, but it was still a comfortable bedroom. The double bed looked inviting with a colorful quilt and plump pillows. There was also a nightstand and dresser and an old bookshelf against the wall. It still held some of the books they had read over the years. An old rocking chair in the corner was the very one she had sat in and rocked Derric when he was a baby. So many good memories were attached to this room. It would be nice to have another boy around. She was happy for

Derric and his sweet wife Becky, but after seeing them over the Christmas holiday, she missed her son more than ever! Keeping up with them via her computer was not the same as having them close by.

Miah worked hard all day. By late afternoon, he had all the wood needed to complete the woodpile on the porch and had started stacking the excess pieces along the shed where Odee had showed him. He worked quietly and steadily, and Odee noticed his determination and saw that he had already chopped most of the logs beside the house. After a quick sandwich for lunch and a glass of homemade lemonade, Odee had helped Miah drag over another log from behind the barn. It had taken both of them to get it moved, and Odee told Miah to take a break. He showed him around the rest of the farm.

It wasn't a big farm, but it was a lot for Odee and Maggie to manage now that Derric was gone, especially since Odee was old-school and wanted to continue farming that way. He wasn't interested in technology and new techniques. He and his son disagreed about this one thing. His way worked, and he was not about to change the way he did things. Stubborn was what Maggie called it, but Derric had not pushed it. He respected his dad too much to argue the point. And his dad provided a great home for him and his mom, so he had no real complaints. Besides, he wasn't really all that excited about farming.

Odee showed Miah the big barn out back that had stalls for their four cows and plenty of dry hay stacked up in the loft. He noticed a small kitten sitting at the edge of the loft, and Odee mentioned that their barn cat just had a new litter. The inside of the barn was very different from the old crumbling barn Miah had slept in the night before. It was clean, dry, and warm, and Miah hoped they would allow him to sleep there if he worked hard. He was more than ready to have a semi-permanent place to stay for a couple of days or even weeks. He needed time to get over Star disappearing and having to cope with abandoning her baby as a result.

In addition to the barn, Odee showed Miah the shed where they milked cows and stored the milk. It was small, but very clean and efficient. Odee explained that they used some of the milk, but a milk truck picked up the rest of it a couple of times a week to be pasteurized. They also had a few distant neighbors who bought milk once a week when they came by for eggs. Nothing went to waste.

There was a chicken coop and a small silo for storing grain. Miah had noticed Maggie carrying a basket and gathering eggs when they passed her to visit the barn. Miah wasn't sure he would enjoy disrupting the chickens to find their eggs, so he hoped that Maggie would continue with that chore.

The afternoon passed quickly as Miah continued splitting the rest of the chunks of wood. He had just picked up the last one and was carefully stacking the pieces along the shed when Maggie came to the door and announced that supper was ready. Odee came out of the barn where he had milked, tethered, and fed the cows for the night. He showed Miah where to place the ax and splitter in the shed and told him they better get inside and wash for supper. As they entered the house, delicious smells of fried chicken and biscuits filled their nostrils. Miah could also smell warm apple pie, and he was sure he must have died and gone to heaven! He put his coat on a hook in the hallway and hurried to the small restroom inside the front door to wash, already anticipating the wonderful meal ahead.

Chapter 5

Odee smiled and shook his head as he waited for the boy to wash; he was thankful for all he had done that day. Odee had been struggling with the ax and keeping up the woodpile due to a lame shoulder that kept bothering him. It was a blessing to have the rest of the wood chopped and stacked. It was certainly more than worth a couple of meals. And Miah could use a little fattening up since he was as thin as a toothpick!

Miah came out of the restroom and hesitated as Odee went in to wash up. Maggie saw him standing there and encouraged him to come into the kitchen and sit where he had that morning. Miah was excited about the hot meal. His mouth was already watering just thinking about it and smelling all the food. Odee came in and sat down at the table just as Maggie was setting down the last bowl of food, which was stacked high with fluffy mashed potatoes. As he had that morning, Odee bowed his head to pray as Maggie took her seat at the table. "Father, we thank you for our many blessings and for all of this food. Thank you for a bountiful harvest, healthy animals, and the extra pair of hands you provided for us today. Keep us always in your loving hands, strengthen us and our faith, and renew all that you promise us, in your Son's holy name. Amen."

Miah felt a little awkward about praying, but he had been exposed to it as a child. He still remembered praying with his mom and attending a small church with her. He had pushed those memories aside because they were too painful, but thought it was interesting that Odee had prayed in a similar manner.

He turned his attention to the wonderful meal in front of him. He took a generous helping of everything passed to him, marveling at the crispy fried chicken and thick, homemade biscuits. He murmured a quick, "Thank you" after every item he took, and Maggie smiled at his excitement. The mashed potatoes were delicious with creamy gravy drizzled over them. Maggie also served a crisp salad and ears of steaming corn on the cob. Miah couldn't believe he was getting all this food at one meal! He had worked hard, and he was hungry!

During his tour of the barn today, Miah noticed a large sign on the outside of the barn that said, "Hewitt Farm." Odee had admitted it was their last name, so now he knew they were Maggie and Odee Hewitt.

Both Odee and Miah ate their food in silence until Maggie finally spoke. "You two must be hungry," she said. "You haven't spoken a word."

"This young man worked hard today; let him eat in peace," Odee responded.

"Sorry, mam," Miah mumbled, "everything is real good." As the men got full, conversation picked up a bit. Odee and Maggie discussed the number of eggs she had gathered that day, and Odee mentioned they had extra milk to sell this week. Miah tried to act casual as he questioned if there was more work they needed help with. He carefully buttered a second biscuit Maggie had pushed his way as he waited for a reply.

Maggie quickly replied that there was always more work than they could handle now that Derric was gone, but Miah noticed the slight scowl Odee shot in her direction.

"Before we talk about more work," he started, "why don't you tell us a little more about yourself, son."

Miah was uneasy, but he had known this was probably coming. He had thought about how he would answer all afternoon. He had to stay as close to the truth as possible without saying enough to make them think they should turn him in or contact authorities. But by the end of the day, he knew he would just go with the truth. He liked this place and would not chance ruining it by lying. Besides, he was tired, hungry, and just wanted to be around good people for a change. If they turned him out for telling the truth, he would just have to move on.

"I was born in Michigan," he started, "but my mother died when I was ten. I was in foster care for years, but nobody really wanted me, and I was passed from place to place. The last home was so horrible I just had to get out of there. At one point, I left and tried to tell one of my teachers, but she told authorities, and eventually they just sent me back. My foster parents didn't feed me much of anything, but I had a couple of friends at school who brought me food. When they figured it out and told me they might pull me out of school, I got scared. I just couldn't take the beatings and hunger, and I knew it would get worse if I was home every day. So, I ran away. I never even understood why they treated me so badly. I swear I tried to do exactly what they wanted. It just wasn't enough." Miah was trembling, but he took a breath and went on.

"I have been moving around and trying to find jobs to get money for food, but I haven't been able to find much. I need a job and a place to stay, but no one wants to hire someone like me, and I have no one to vouch for me. Once they see me in my worn clothes and find out I have no references, they just aren't interested in hiring me. I can promise you I will not steal anything, and I will work hard. I just need someone to believe in me and give me a chance."

Miah was getting choked up as the words poured out, and he noticed Maggie had tears in her eyes as well. He had probably just ruined his chances of staying here, but he had held it all inside for so long. And while he stuck with the truth, he still couldn't tell them about the baby. It was all too much, and any time he thought about or mentioned his mom, he cried. He missed her so much, and somehow all those feelings had been tied up with the baby.

As Miah sat there thinking he had ruined his chances with the Hewitts, Odee got up from the table and came around to sit next to him. He took Miah's hands in his own and would not let the startled boy pull away. He looked Miah in the eyes and told him he was sorry—sorry for the loss of his mom, sorry for the way other families had treated him, and sorry for the way he'd had to live on the run. When the boy started sobbing, he put his arms around him and hugged him. No one had hugged him since his mother died.

When Miah finally stopped crying, Odee sat back, keeping Miah's hands in his own. "Let me pray with you, son," he said. "Heavenly Father, hear our prayers for this young man. He has been on his own for a long time, but he needs a home. Show us how to handle this situation and help us to show this boy that *you* are our hope and our strength. Lead us on the path that you created us to follow and be ever present as we try to follow your direction. We prayed for help, and this young man showed up at our doorstep. Show us the way to helping one another. We pray all of this in your name. Amen."

When Odee let go of Miah's hands and Miah looked up, he saw that Maggie had been praying with them. She rushed over to give Miah a hug and tell him it was going to be okay. Odee went back to his seat at the table, and Maggie went over to the counter and brought back a warm apple pie.

As they were eating pie, Odee and Maggie kept looking at Miah, making him feel uncomfortable. He finished the delicious dessert and finally took matters into his own hands. "I know you have to be shocked,"

Miah started, "but I wanted you to know the truth. I appreciate all that you have given me today, the job and especially the three meals. It's the best food I have tasted since my mom died, and this day has been more than I ever hoped for. If you could find it in your hearts to let me sleep in your barn tonight, I will be on my way first thing in the morning. The last thing I want to be is a problem for you."

Maggie startled Miah by jumping up quickly and stating in a no-nonsense tone: "You will do nothing of the sort, young man! We have a perfectly fine and very empty bedroom upstairs you are welcome to use for as long as you want. There will be no sleeping in the barn and no leaving unless you want to!"

"Now Maggie," Odee added. "Don't scare the boy to death. He just got here. He has worked hard all day and doesn't need us terrifying him to boot." He looked at Miah and continued. "Why don't you get a good night's sleep, and we can talk about everything in the morning. Does that work for you? I suggest that you sleep in the bedroom instead of the barn . . . it's much warmer and will be a lot more comfortable. Our son slept there for years and seemed to enjoy it, so I think you will, too. What do you say?"

Miah looked from Odee to Maggie and saw nothing but kindness. He didn't know what tomorrow would bring, but he was tired of trying to figure it out. A good night's sleep on a real bed would be heaven. He knew without a doubt he would be safe here, and Odee's prayers had given him hope. He nodded his head yes.

Chapter 6

Maggie went to work picking up the dessert dishes and shooing the men away. She suggested
that Odee show Miah upstairs where he could take a
hot shower and get ready for bed. As they climbed the
stairs, Miah took in every detail. They came to a nar-
row hallway with three doors. Odee opened the middle
door to show Miah a small bathroom with a shower,
sink, and toilet, and he took a moment to show Miah
how the shower worked. He opened the cupboard in
one corner to show the boy clean towels and wash-
cloths, soap, shampoo, extra toilet paper, and a variety
of medicines and other toiletries.

On either side of the bathroom door, were doors to the bedrooms. Odee opened the one on the right to show Miah his son Derric's old room. It was a generous room, containing a bed and nightstand, dresser, bookcase, and rocking chair. Odee walked over to the closet to show Miah some clothes Derric didn't want and had left behind. He told the boy he was welcome to anything that fit, pulling a pair of cotton pajamas from the shelf inside he thought would do for sleeping. Miah thought they looked a little big for him, but a hot shower and any clean clothing would be a pleasant change. Odee suggested he go ahead and get in the shower, noticing the boy was looking more exhausted by the moment. He told him he would bring his backpack up and put it in the bedroom.

Miah took the pajamas and headed into the small bathroom. He really was exhausted. The long walk this morning and the hard work all day had worn him out completely. He took a wonderfully hot shower, using the soap to clean his hair as well, and dried off with a clean towel. He stepped into the baggy pajamas, still thankful for them despite their size. He hung the towel carefully over the rod at the end of the shower and scrubbed his teeth with his finger. He had a toothbrush but it was in his backpack, and he was too tired to worry about it. He picked up his filthy clothing intending to carry it back to the bedroom. As he came out of the bathroom, Odee was returning up the stairs with his backpack, and Maggie was right behind him. Miah took the backpack with one hand, holding up the pajamas with the other. He was embarrassed about the fit and trying to carry the dirty clothes with the same hand. Maggie saved him by taking the dirty clothes from him gently, telling him she would wash them when she did laundry that night. Miah knew it was still early, but he was too tired for any more conversation. After uttering a quick thank you, he said good night and started toward the bedroom. He could hardly wait to get into a real bed for a change! He placed his backpack on the dresser, quickly turned out the light, and crawled into bed. He was asleep the moment his head hit the soft, fluffy, *clean* pillow.

The next morning, Miah awoke to the wonderful smell of cinnamon rolls! His tummy was already growling as he eagerly scrambled out of bed and into the spare clothes he pulled from his backpack. He folded the pajamas carefully and placed them back in the closet where Odee had found them. Finding his toothbrush in his backpack, he rushed into the bathroom, scrubbed his face, brushed his teeth, and was quickly ready for a new day. He made his bed up neatly and sat his backpack in the rocking chair. He couldn't remember a time when he was so excited for what would come in the day ahead, and having delicious food cooked and placed in front of him was a wonderful new experience.

Odee and Maggie were already in the kitchen chatting and drinking coffee when Miah got downstairs. He joined them at the table where Maggie placed a steaming cup of hot cocoa in front of him with a smile. "Good morning," she said. "I hope you slept well. Would you like a roll before you start chores?"

"The bed was comfortable, and I slept very well," Miah answered politely, noticing that Odee was devouring a large homemade cinnamon roll. "A roll would be great."

Maggie went over to the stove and scooped one up from the pan, placing it on a plate and bringing it back to the table. "I'll make a heartier breakfast a little later," she told Miah. "This will hold you till then."

"Wow, thank you," Miah replied as he picked up the roll that was still warm from the oven and dripping with icing. He just shook his head as he tasted the unexpected treat, and Maggie smiled and patted his shoulder as she sat back down to finish her coffee.

Miah heard the Hewitts talking about their plans for the day as he finished his roll and cocoa. He was eager to show them how much he could help around the farm. He desperately wanted to stay with them for a while. Not having to worry about where he was going to stay and what he could find to eat was a dream for him. He had to make this work. He just had to!

When Odee finished his coffee, he told Miah it was time to do the morning chores and added with a smile, "That is if you are staying?" Miah nodded yes and jumped up quickly, ready to get started! He heard Maggie laughing as they headed out the door.

One of the morning chores consisted of milking the cows in the milking shed, feeding them, and getting them out to pasture. Odee showed Miah how to attach the milking machines to the cows and how to remove them when they were full. They also had to manually dump the milk into the storage tank. Once the storage tank was more than half-full, the milk went into large containers that were then placed in the cooler for their own use and for selling to neighbors. Odee explained that milking had to be done twice a day, morning and night. Once the cows were out in the field, the milking area had to be hosed down thoroughly for the next milking.

In the barn, there were additional chores. The stalls where the cows slept had to be cleaned, and more hay had to be pitched into the clean stalls from the loft. The feed and water troughs had to be filled as well. It was hard work, but Miah enjoyed it. It was actually nice to have an adult talk to him and tell him what to do in a pleasant, non-critical way. Odee was free with praise as well and complimented Miah when he picked up quickly on how to do the chores. A comfortable atmosphere developed between them as they chatted and worked together. Miah mentioned the old barn he had slept in, and Odee told him it had been there as long as he could remember. He added that it was a wonder it was still standing.

As soon as the chores were completed, they headed back in for the breakfast Maggie had promised. Scrambled eggs and sausage awaited them, and once again, Odee said a prayer before they ate. Miah folded his hands and bowed his head, and as Odee prayed, he began to hope that God was really there and had not given up on him yet.

During breakfast, Odee mentioned that the fence in the pasture needed repair. When they finished eating, they headed outside to get materials. Odee took Miah back to the shed where he had stored the axe and splitter and showed him a large toolbox that held everything they needed. After gathering hammers and nails and a spool of wire, they headed toward the pasture. There was a large fenced-in area behind the barn where the cows wandered during the day, munching grass in the spring, summer, and fall, and the large pile of hay in the corner provided for them during the winter months. Once they got closer, Miah could see that a section of fence had weathered and split in a couple of places. He helped Odee pull the fence rails back in place and hammer nails in to hold them. For extra support, they wrapped wire around the repaired area. After repairing all the broken fence rails, they headed back to the shed to put the tools away. They spent the rest of day with normal tasks around the farm. They swept the barn and pulled additional bales of hay from under a tarp behind the barn where they had been piled to use during the winter. Miah got a few minutes to play with the litter of kittens when he took hay up to the loft, and Odee gave him a dish to fill with milk from the milk shed for them. Miah had seen many stray animals during his time on the run, but nothing as cute as the five little kittens. He marveled at their different colors and praised the mama cat for taking such good care of her babies.

Maggie brought them sandwiches for lunch, and they spent the afternoon hauling more logs from the woods at the back of their property. These were pulled over to where Miah had chopped wood the day before so they would be ready to chop as the wood supply depleted. Odee also showed Miah the winding path that led down to mailbox at the end of their drive. He picked up the mail, and they carried it back to the house just as Maggie opened the door to tell them supper was almost ready. Once again, they washed up as they had the night before in preparation for supper. Miah thought he could smell spaghetti and meatballs and could hardly wait to eat. His stomach had already accustomed itself to three meals per day, and the hard work burned it off as quickly as he took it in, so it was growling in anticipation. He could still hardly believe this was real.

Chapter 7

The days passed quickly, and soon a week had flown by. Miah got accustomed to the hard work and wonderful food. He was still very thankful and helped Odee and Maggie with whatever they needed. In addition to helping Odee with the chores, he swept and mopped the kitchen for Maggie and made sure to keep the wood container by the fireplace full. The pleasant atmosphere relaxed the boy, and his personality began to emerge. No one had shown him an ounce of positive attention since his mother had died. He was kind and inquisitive; he learned quickly and was a good listener. Sometimes in the evening, he would sit for a while with Maggie and Odee and listen to their stories about Derric or something that had happened on the farm.

One evening, Maggie went upstairs with Miah and insisted he go through Derric's closet and see if there were items that would fit him. When they came across a couple of things close to his size, she set them aside explaining she would alter them to fit him better. When he resisted, she scolded him and told him he needed more than one change of clothing. She said she had been meaning to box up the items and get rid of them anyway, so he was actually helping her if he could use some of it. She even suggested he look through the books on the bookshelf and help himself to anything he found interesting. She told him to place his things in the empty dresser drawers rather than trying to stuff everything in his backpack. It wasn't as if anyone else needed the space. Sheepishly, he did as she asked, noticing that she still got a little emotional about the fact that Derric had grown and gone. More than anything, he wanted to please this woman who continued to overwhelm him with the generosity and kindness she lavished on him daily.

On Saturday, after the morning chores, Odee told Miah that he needed to go into town to get a few supplies and asked if he would like to tag along. When Miah said he would rather stay home and help Maggie with things around the house, he knew the boy was still worried about someone seeing him and asking questions. What he didn't realize was that Miah was also worried that somehow he would get the Hewitts in trouble. He would leave them before he let that happen. Besides, he wanted the time to surprise Odee by fixing the part of the front porch that sagged. Now that he had helped Odee repair the fence in the pasture, he was pretty sure he could crawl underneath the porch and fix the boards that had split. He hoped he could figure it all out while Odee was gone.

Odee left right after breakfast, and Miah told Maggie he needed to finish a couple of chores. Heading outside to the shed, he retrieved the hammer and nails from the toolbox Odee had shown him, along with the spool of wire. Crawling under the front porch, he could see where a couple of boards supporting the porch had started to split. Lying on the ice-cold ground, he was thankful for the warmer coat Maggie had almost demanded he start using. Derric had hardly worn it, but it was the nicest coat Miah could ever remember wearing. Carefully, he wrapped a piece of the wire around the split board to hold it in place while he nailed it together. By the time he had repeated the process along the entire end of the porch, he could actually see it lifting back up into place. He found a couple of other loose boards that would have eventually split as well and nailed them back to the support beam. Once he examined everything he could see, he slid back out from under the porch to admire his work.

The improvement was astonishing! The porch no longer sagged on one end. Taking the tools back to the shed, he replaced them where he had found them and headed out to the barn to play with the kittens for a bit. When he climbed up to the loft and sat in the hay, the kittens came out from hiding to greet him. He petted each of them, including the mama cat. She had gotten used to having him around her little brood. He picked up his favorite, a tiny calico, and gave her a special hug.

Then he headed back down the loft ladder and went inside to see if he could help Maggie.

When he got inside, he could smell fresh-baked cookies. *Oatmeal raisin*, he thought, as he hung his coat on the hook in the hallway. Sure enough, Maggie was just pulling out the last batch of cookies as he came into the kitchen. She smiled at Miah and put a couple on a plate for each of them. "How about a couple of warm cookies and a glass of milk," she said to Miah.

"I was going to see if I could sweep and mop for you again," Miah offered.

"Well you don't have to work every second," Maggie replied. "I heard you out there hammering away. Take a break and have some cookies with me."

Miah wasn't going to argue. The cookies and milk sounded good. He took his seat beside her and sat down to enjoy the treat. Maggie and Miah chatted easily about things around the farm, and Maggie told him how much she appreciated all the help he was providing Odee. He never complained, but she knew it was getting harder and harder for Odee to keep up with everything. It led to her mentioning the disappointment

Odee had felt when Derric went away to college, although she was quick to add that he would never keep their son from following his dreams of becoming a computer analyst. As much as Derric had been willing to help around the farm, it wasn't hard to see that his heart just wasn't in it. He spent every extra second on his computer. In fact, she told Miah, there is probably still a computer upstairs in his closet. I don't know if you use computers or not, but you are welcome to try it. We have Internet access here because I have a laptop and keep up with my son and his wife that way. Derric bought a computer just before he left, but I don't think there was anything wrong with his old one. He just wanted the latest and greatest technology. He excelled in college and has a wonderful job with a large computer firm in San Francisco. While Miah could hear the pride in her voice, he also saw the sadness that came from knowing her son was so far away.

Miah had used computers in school, but he had never had one of his own. He and Star had played around on one in the library one day when they had nothing better to do. He told Maggie he would look and see if he could figure out how to use it. She mentioned that their church offered classes on a variety of topics and beginning computers was one of them. She told him that was how Odee learned to keep track of farm supplies and said that he was actually quite good at manipulating data, especially on spreadsheets.

Then she got personal. "What do you want to do with your life," she asked Miah out of the blue.

"Um, I haven't really had time to think about it," Miah replied. "I liked reading and writing in school, but since I have been out of school for a while, I haven't gotten a lot of practice. I have been looking through some of Derric's books, and I really enjoy reading when I have the time. I would love to be able to focus on getting the rest of my high school education. I will be sixteen at the end of the month, and I know I am way behind, but I was always in advanced classes in school, and I learn quickly. I would like to try if you are really okay with me using the computer."

Maggie reassured him and told him to let her know if he couldn't get it working, but she was pretty sure it was still in good shape. She admitted that she had been a teacher herself many years ago and had kept up learning on-line thanks to help from her son. She told him she would be happy to sit down with him and show him some classes he could take on the computer. Most education was available on-line now if he was really interested. Then she caught him off guard with her next question.

"What day is your birthday, Miah?" she asked.

"Oh, it's January twenty-seventh," he replied. "No big deal though, just another day for me." He seemed a bit embarrassed, so she let it go. She wondered how long it had been since anyone had acknowledged this boy's birthday and started planning for the occasion at that very moment. He would certainly have a birthday celebration this year!

Chapter 8

Miah tried not to get too excited, but the thought of being able to catch up with his schooling made his heart soar! He only hoped this was not too good to be true. He made up his mind at that moment to start praying at night. If people like the Hewitts believed God answered their prayers, there must be something to it. He knew his mother believed, too, so it was time he tried something different. He could use the Bible in Derric's room, so he would start that very night!

After they devoured the cookies and milk, Miah insisted on sweeping and mopping the kitchen for Maggie. His years in foster homes had taught him many things, including how to keep a home spotless. It wasn't long before the kitchen floor was clean and shiny.

Maggie took advantage of her break from the kitchen to get on her computer and connect with her son. She sent him a long message about Miah and the circumstances surrounding his being there. Derric cautioned her to be careful, but Maggie knew that if her son met Miah he would take to him as easily as they had. She asked Derric again if there was anything in his room he wanted her to save and got the negative answer she expected. Derric had always been a kind, generous person and told her the kid was welcome to anything he had left behind. He told his mom that he and Becky hoped to get home to visit them in the spring or summer and might even have a big surprise for them. Always happy to have conversation with her son, Maggie signed off the computer in much better spirits.

Odee returned from town shortly after Miah had finished the kitchen. Miah went outside and helped him unload the supplies he had purchased. When he saw the porch was no longer sagging at one end, he was amazed Miah had figured out how to repair it on his own. He told him what a great job he had done, thankful for one less thing to do. Dinner that night was lighthearted and fun. Maggie had prepared a meatloaf and baked potatoes with a warm apple cake for dessert. She was extremely pleased with the yarn Odee had purchased for her in town so she could finish a project she was working on. Everyone seemed at ease and happy, and Miah was starting to get used to the full, satisfied feeling of a well-fed teenager.

Later that night after telling the Hewitts he was turning in early and promising to go to church with them in the morning, he got out the Bible he had seen on the bookshelf. As he opened it, a piece of paper fell out. Picking it up, he saw it was a list of verses addressing daily issues people faced throughout life. There was a column of issues with corresponding verses to read in the Bible for encouragement. He turned the paper over, and on the back were definitions of particular words used in the Bible. The first one was *grace*. Someone had written the definition after the word. It said, "Grace: God's gift to believers." Miah wasn't sure what that meant. Turning the page back over, he looked down the list of words with corresponding verses until he came to the word *hopelessness*. Feeling as if he certainly knew what that was about, he turned to the first verse in the Bible that was supposed to offer encouragement.

> Praise be to the God and Father of our Lord Jesus Christ! In his great mercy he has given us new birth into a living hope through the resurrection of Jesus Christ from the dead, and into an inheritance that can never perish, spoil or fade. This inheritance is kept in heaven for you, who through faith are shielded by God's power until the coming of the salvation that is ready to be revealed in the last time. In all this you greatly rejoice, though now for a little while you may have had to suffer grief in all kinds of trials. (1 Peter 1:3–6 NIV)

Miah read the verse a couple of times. Was the Bible saying that if you believe in Jesus Christ, you could go to heaven no matter what had happened in your life? Was it possible that God was always there even when horrible things were happening? He couldn't stop reading. The next verse said:

> The Lord delights in those who fear him, who put their hope in his unfailing love. (Ps. 147:11 NIV)

Fear God? That didn't seem right. This was really confusing. He looked up the last verse.

> Through whom we have gained access by faith into this grace in which we now stand. And we boast in the hope of the glory of God. Not only so, but we also glory in our sufferings, because we know that suffering produces perseverance; perseverance, character; and character, hope. And hope does not put us to shame, because God's love has been poured out into our hearts through the Holy Spirit, who has been given to us. You see, at just the right time, when we were still powerless, Christ died for the ungodly. (Rom. 5:2–6 NIV)

Glory in our sufferings? How did that make any sense? Miah folded the paper, placed it back in the Bible, and returned it to the shelf. He had so many questions about God, but he didn't think he would ever find the answers. Still, that word *hope* kept reminding him of his mother and her insistence that there is always hope. But it was too hard to understand how he could be someone God loved. He didn't think God would want someone like him as part of his family, especially after he abandoned the baby. Miah didn't want anything to do with any more sufferings, either. He had suffered enough since his mother died, hadn't he?

Miah climbed into bed, still wearing the borrowed pajamas. He wondered what he was doing here at this farm and what he hoped for. He didn't know. He had come here for something to eat and drink, hoping to find a job and a place to sleep. Had God been part of bringing him here? He had certainly received more than he hoped for when he walked up those steps. Hope, hope, hope. The word seemed to be everywhere! Still, he thought again about the little baby girl he had left on a doorstep. Tears filled his eyes as he concluded that even God would have a hard time forgiving him for that!

Chapter 9

The smell of breakfast woke Miah up bright and early the next morning. He quietly used the restroom and brushed his teeth, having already showered the night before. Looking through the clothing Maggie had laundered, altered, and hung in the closet, he chose a pair of khaki pants and a button-down shirt to wear to church. Once he had dressed, he put his pajamas back in the drawer, combed his curly hair, and headed down to see what was for breakfast. He was sure he could smell pancakes in the making!

Odee and Maggie were already in the kitchen, and breakfast was almost ready. It was blueberry pancakes and sausage this morning, and Miah was starving after his early night to bed. He was a bit quiet as he ate, thinking about church and the people he was about meet. He was worried that someone would guess that he did not belong with people like the Hewitts.

The small, white church was very similar to the one Miah remembered attending with his mother. The Hewitts introduced him to people in the congregation and eventually to the pastor. They told everyone he was their friend and was helping Odee out at the farm, since Derric had moved away. Everyone, including the pastor, thanked him for helping them out.

Miah sat quietly listening to the service. He heard the pastor talking about putting your faith in God no matter what happened and learning to talk to Him as if He were a loving father. Miah wasn't sure how to do that since he had never had a father, but he would like to know that there was always someone there for him. Looking over at Odee and Maggie, he wanted to think they would always be there for him, but he knew it wasn't reasonable. They had no reason to keep him around, except for the help they needed on the farm. As much as he hoped they cared for him like he did them, he knew from experience that it could disappear in a heartbeat—just like his mom. He felt the sadness trickle into his soul as the pastor finished the service.

On January 27, Miah woke up with the sudden realization that he was sixteen years old! He looked around the room and marveled at all he had. While most boys his age were thinking about girls and getting their drivers licenses, Miah was simply happy to have a warm place to stay, regular meals, and people around him who seemed to care. Feeling lucky and thinking that maybe he could ask Odee to teach *him* to drive someday, he whistled happily as he got in the shower.

Downstairs, Maggie was bustling about making sure everything would be perfect for dinner that evening. She had gone into town with Odee the week before, wanting to pick up a couple of things for her surprise. They had found a beautiful Bible to give Miah, and she had picked up everything she needed for the big day. She was so excited she could hardly contain it, and even Odee seemed happy to be part of giving him a special day.

When Miah got downstairs, he was pleasantly surprised to see that Maggie had made him the cinnamon rolls he had liked so much when he first tried them. She gave him a warm hug and told him happy birthday. She had already asked him a few days earlier what he would like for his birthday dinner, and though he had said anything was fine, he mentioned that her fried chicken and biscuits were a favorite of his! She smiled and said she thought she could handle that.

As he and Odee put on their coats to head out for chores, Odee handed him a brand-new hat in bright red. It had warm fleece on the inside, and Miah thought it was the nicest hat he had ever had. He put it on immediately, thanking Odee over and over.

"Happy birthday, Miah," Odee said with a hug. "You didn't think we would forget, did you?"

Miah was speechless and hugged Odee back, noticing that Maggie was watching them from the kitchen door. His spirits soared as he thought about the kindness they continued to show him, and Maggie prayed they could keep this boy who worked so hard and appreciated every little thing. She could hardly wait for their dinner celebration as she hurried back to the kitchen to make his birthday cake!

Dinner that night topped even the first meal Miah had experienced with them. Everything was more than he had hoped for, and Miah could sense both Odee and Maggie's excitement. He thought he smelled cake when he came inside, and after dinner, he discovered he was right. But nothing prepared him for what came next. After clearing the dinner plates, Maggie set out dessert plates as Odee disappeared into the small room off the kitchen. As Maggie fiddled with napkins and clean silverware, Odee came back carrying the biggest cake Miah had ever seen! It was three layers high, with dark chocolate frosting and sixteen lighted candles. Before Miah could say a word, Maggie and Odee started singing happy birthday. Miah looked from one to the other and he almost cried. At the end of the song, Maggie patted him on the back and said, "Make a wish and blow out the candles!"

Miah was embarrassed and happy at the same time. He closed his eyes, and without hesitation, he wished to stay with the Hewitts forever. Maggie and Odee laughed at his expression of surprise and told him they were very happy to celebrate his birthday with him. After taking off the blown-out candles, Maggie cut Miah a huge slice of the rich, chocolate cake and added a big scoop of vanilla ice cream from the container Odee brought over from the freezer. Miah thought he had died and gone to heaven again when he took the first bite. He could not remember the last time he had a birthday like this. As they were finishing the wonderful birthday dessert, Maggie got up and brought over a package that had been sitting out of sight on the counter and handed it to Miah. "This is from me and Odee," she said. "We are so happy to have you here with us, Miah. I hope you like it."

Now Miah was really embarrassed. "You shouldn't have done this," he said with concern. "The meal and the cake were enough."

"Nonsense," Odee spoke up. "It's your birthday; there is supposed to be cake and ice cream and presents."

As Miah opened the gift, he found a beautiful, leather-bound Bible. Inside the cover was his name and date of birth and it said simply: "For Miah, from the Hewitt family." There was also a folded advertisement with a picture of various types of boots. "We want you to pick out a pair," Maggie stated.

"You can't keep wearing those ragged sneakers around the farm," Odee added. "You need a pair of boots."

Miah just kept looking at the piece of paper and the expensive-looking boots. This time he couldn't stop the tears from welling up in his eyes. "It's too much," he mumbled.

"It isn't," Odee replied quietly. You have helped me for weeks around the farm without one complaint. You have listened and learned and done everything I asked you to do and more. You fixed the porch, and you help Maggie without ever being asked. You deserve it son, and we love having you around. Please let us do this for you."

Miah looked at Odee as he finished speaking and over at Maggie who was so excited about his birthday. His eyes showed his appreciation, and he couldn't stop the tears that slid down his cheeks. "I will never forget this," he said, "*never!*"

"Well, which ones do you like," Maggie asked as she came over behind Miah and pointed at the paper. "Brown or black, short or tall?" she asked.

Miah pointed out a pair of rugged-looking brown boots, and Maggie told him that those were her favorite as well and asked him his size. Then she snatched the paper and making a couple of notes on it, she tucked it in her apron pocket. Odee and Miah laughed and helped Maggie clear the table. Maggie insisted that Miah go in the living room and check out his new Bible while they cleaned up. Feeling like an excited child, Miah took the Bible and did as he was told.

Chapter 10

The second week in February, Miah walked into the kitchen one to day to find Maggie making heart-shaped cookies. He watched as she took two of the cooled cookies and carefully spread a red mixture in between them, sticking them together. She laid them on waxed paper with others she had finished and carefully sifted powdered sugar over them. "Would you like to try one?" she asked Miah as she handed him a finished cookie. Of course, he could not refuse!

"Umm . . . raspberry, these are wonderful," Miah told Maggie. "Why are you making them?"

"It's Valentine's Day," Maggie replied. "I always make a special treat for Odee to show him I love him.

Everybody treats their loved ones on Valentine's Day! These are for you, too!"

Miah vaguely remembered giving his mom a small, heart-shaped box of chocolates when he was younger. He had almost forgotten what holidays were like. He mumbled a quick thank you for the cookie and headed outside. What could he do for Maggie and Odee to show them he cared about them? He thought about it all day and finally he came up with something. Maggie had mentioned that they needed to get some coasters for their drinks. She hated making water rings on the tables at either end of the sofa. Maybe he could make some! He had seen some scrap wood out behind the barn, so he headed in that direction. Odee was busy inside helping Maggie with something, so they wouldn't miss him. He found a couple of small, square pieces of wood and got to work. Using a piece of sandpaper from the shed, he carefully sanded all the edges until they were smooth and almost round. Taking a small, pointed tool he found in the toolbox, he etched a large H in the center of each square. Once he was satisfied there were no rough spots, he put everything back and headed inside. Going upstairs, he went in his room and closed the door. From the closet, he pulled out a set of permanent markers he had noticed. Sitting on the edge of the bed, he took the squares of light brown wood one at a time and filled in the thick H he had carved in the center of each with black ink. He thought they looked pretty good, but they needed something for Valentine's Day. Carefully, he drew small hearts in each corner, varying the color from pink to dark red. Satisfied with the results, he found some red tissue paper and tape in the closet and wrapped them up. Not perfect, but not too bad. Hearing Maggie call out that supper was ready, he picked up his package and headed downstairs.

When he sat down at the table, he noticed a big vase of red roses in the center, which Maggie proudly told him Odee had given her for Valentine's Day. He placed the package on the empty chair next to him. He would surprise them with it after dinner. Maggie had made a wonderful supper tonight: a large roast beef with little carrots and potatoes. Rich, dark gravy topped it off and more of the wonderful homemade bread. Afterward,

Maggie brought out the delicious heart-shaped cookies she had made with the mouth-watering raspberry filling. "For Valentine's Day," she said, and Odee looked at them with appreciation. As they were all enjoying the special cookies, Miah reached down and brought up the little package he had put together.

"Just a little something for Valentine's Day for both of you," he mumbled. He watched as Maggie took off the tissue paper and showed Odee the coasters he had made. "It isn't much," he offered. "I made them myself. Maggie is always saying she needs a couple of them for the end tables." He was embarrassed by now and was wishing he hadn't done anything when Maggie got up and came around the table to give him a hug.

"They're perfect," she told Miah. "Thank you; it was so thoughtful of you." Maggie sat back down at the table, and Miah noticed Odee was holding one of the coasters.

"Good job," he said to Miah, "Thank you, son." He picked up the coasters and walked into the living room where he placed one on each of the end tables. Miah went to bed that evening still glowing from the praise.

Days turned into weeks at the farm, and before he knew it, spring was on its way. Miah had eased into life on the farm like it was meant for him. He had grown more and more fond of Odee and Maggie, and they treated him like a son. He finally had a family of sorts, and he was happier than he had been in a long time. Maggie had helped him log onto educational sites on the computer Derric had left in his room. He was taking classes on-line now and had almost caught up to where he would be if he were in school. He could go faster on the computer, and Maggie had told him she was confident he could graduate within a year if he kept up the good work! He certainly didn't lack for intelligence despite what some of his foster parents had told him. Maggie was a wonderful teacher, and Miah envied the students she had taught in the past. He was determined to put in the time on his schooling, even if it meant doing it at night when Maggie and Odee were sleeping.

Spring brought a new excitement to the farm when Odee discovered one of his cows was expecting. He had borrowed a bull from a friend at church, and the result had been positive. Miah was awed at her growing tummy and the idea of being part of the birth. Odee had explained everything that would happen during the birth and was thankful that Miah would be there to assist. He could hardly wait to see what the calf would look like.

Derric and Becky were coming out for a visit in April, during Easter, and Miah was feeling anxious about meeting them. He had helped Odee clean out the spare room at the back of the house, and set up new furniture they had ordered. It was a little bigger than the bedroom upstairs, and Maggie said it would be better for their old bones not to have to navigate the stairs. She mentioned they had wanted to do it for years, but it was just too much for them to handle without help. She had ordered new bedding, curtains, and a rug, and Odee smiled and shook his head as she bustled around getting everything just right. Miah was happy for them, and enjoyed watching the transformation of the room. He helped Maggie clean the bedroom upstairs once she got everything in the new bedroom, sprucing it up in preparation for Derric coming back.

Miah offered to move his things in to the other bedroom so Derric could have his own room, but Maggie said it wasn't necessary. Besides, their old room was larger, which would give Derric and Becky a little more room. Miah could tell she was super excited for them to visit. He just hoped Derric would not be upset about him being there.

Miah was beginning to feel like he knew Derric a bit since he was staying in his room and heard stories about his childhood. Still, he also knew Derric must have been wondering about him showing up at the farm and then moving in. He understood how that must look and felt apprehensive, but he couldn't help but be a little excited at the same time.

Chapter 11

Miah had been at the farm for two full months when Odee approached him right after the milk truck picked up the milk one morning. He was beaming because the amount of milk had brought extra money the last couple of weeks. With the new cow coming, things were looking really good. "I want to talk to you about all of your help around the farm," he said. "I want to compensate you on a regular basis for all the work you are doing."

Miah was immediately concerned. "No," he said. "That isn't necessary, Odee! I love it here at the farm, and you and Maggie have done so much for me. I don't want money, too! I am happy to help in return for a place to stay and meals. I know it must cost more with me living and eating here, and that is enough. Besides, you have been buying me things, too. I love the new boots Maggie ordered and the Bible you got me the last time you went to town. That's enough." Odee saw that he was getting upset.

"Look," he told Miah, "I was to a point where I was going to have to hire someone to help me. I couldn't manage this place on my own. Maggie and I have done well over the years, and we didn't need all the money we saved for Derric's college education because he earned scholarships. We are doing great financially, and some of that is because of all your help. I don't want to argue with you about this. Maggie and I have discussed what we think is a fair amount of money for what you do, and we are in agreement on this. We insist on putting a little bit aside for you each week for wages. I have a lock box you can keep in your room if you don't want to go to the bank right now. You work hard around here, and you deserve it. I will put it in a sealed envelope at the end of each week, and you can just put it in the lock-box if you want."

"But, Odee," Miah started.

"No buts," Odee said firmly. "If you don't want to use the money, that's up to you, but we are still going to give it to you. You are going to need it one day. If you weren't staying here you would have to get a job somewhere else in order to survive, and we don't want you to do that. I love having you around the place. Can you understand that? Now let's get the rest of the chores done."

Miah nodded, but the concerned look remained on his face throughout the day. He prayed that night for understanding and guidance. He had gotten in the habit of picking out a Scripture to read each night before he went to bed in an effort to learn more about God and understand the Sunday sermons better. When he was on the computer in the evening, he would look up a verse from the Bible he thought fit the day and write it down. Then he would get out his new Bible and read it.

Tonight, he looked for a verse about understanding. In Proverbs, he found:

A person may think their own ways are right, but the Lord weighs the heart. (Prov. 21:2 NIV)

He pondered that for a moment, but it was the second verse he found that really got his attention.

Call to me and I will answer you and tell you great and unsearchable things you do not know. (Jer. 33:3 NIV)

Miah was convinced this was speaking directly to him, especially since it came from the book of Jeremiah (his own name). He simply needed to reach out to God for an answer. But how was he supposed to do that? Was it as simple as saying a prayer? Well, he would give it a try.

Listening to Odee pray continued to remind him of praying with his mom. Those were good memories, so he decided it was time he tried it again. Getting down on his knees, as if he remembered doing with his mom, he began to pray.

"Dear God, please help me to understand why Odee and Maggie want to give me money to work for them. I am so happy with all they already provide me. Why do they feel the need to give me money for helping them? Does it mean they want to think of me as an employee rather than a member of their family? I love them Lord, and I want them to know that just being here means the world to me. I don't know why they want to give me money, but please help me to understand. Thanks for listening to me. Amen."

As Miah crawled into bed, he felt better. He didn't know if God would answer him or if he would even recognize it if he did, but it felt better just talking to Him.

March came and went, and Maggie got more excited as the day of Derric and Becky's arrival drew near. They were supposed to arrive on Good Friday, and as the three of them went to church that morning, Miah could sense the anticipation. Despite the distraction, Odee was careful to explain Good Friday to Miah and make sure he understood the whole Easter celebration. He was happy that Miah seemed almost as interested in learning about the Bible as he was in completing his schooling. They'd had many conversations about God and the Bible in the last couple of weeks.

They hadn't been home from church very long when Miah heard a vehicle pull up out front and knew Derric and Becky had arrived. He hung back as Maggie threw open the door and rushed out to greet them with Odee right on her heels.

Derric was about average height and weight with brown hair and brown eyes. He hugged his mom tightly and turned to give his dad a hug while his mom turned to Becky. Becky was much smaller but also had brown hair and eyes. They both seemed very happy to see the Hewitts. As soon as the initial greetings were over, Odee pulled Miah forward to be introduced.

"This is Miah," Odee stated proudly. "He is the young man who has been helping out at the farm the last couple of months." Miah shyly shook Derric's hand as he reached out with his own, and Becky surprised him with a warm hug. Maggie began to hustle them all inside, while Odee turned to help Derric carry in their bags. Noticing there were additional bags, Miah picked up a bag as well and headed inside. As Derric followed, he turned toward Odee with a smile of appreciation.

Derric had called Odee after hearing about Miah from his mom, worried about them allowing a stranger into their home. Odee had filled him in with the details Miah had provided them and Derric had done a little research of his own. He was able to verify the death of Miah's mother and had also discovered that his father had died previously while serving in the Army. He wondered if Miah even knew that, and his heart went out to this young man who had managed to survive in spite of losing both parents by the time he was ten years old. He knew it hadn't been easy for the kid because Odee had also told him about the foster homes and being on the run. Thankfully, he had already turned sixteen and Derric was pretty sure he wouldn't be forced to return to foster care especially if he was managing on his own. Still, Derric was thankful Maggie and Odee had already been foster parents years ago and could probably be reinstated if necessary. He certainly didn't want the poor kid to have to go on the run again. There were good foster parents, too; his own parents were a great example, but he was pretty sure he would never convince Miah of that. The key was to keep him happy and busy here on the farm while he prepared for his future. He was pleased to hear from his mom that Miah was working on finishing his schooling. That would help. He was also happy to hear about how much he was helping around the farm. It might be nice to have a "little brother" around for a change. He would make sure Miah had a way to reach him so he could get another perspective on how his parents were doing.

Once inside with all the bags carried upstairs, they all sat down to visit. Maggie brought out a plate of cookies and lemonade, and soon they were all chatting away and laughing. Derric asked Miah about school and church and was happy to hear he was enjoying both. Miah thanked him for letting him use his room and for all of things he had left behind. Derric put Miah's nervousness about it all to rest, telling him he was glad none of it was going to waste. He offered to show Miah a couple of things on the computer that would make studying a bit easier, and Becky warned him jokingly about not letting him touch a computer or they would never see him again.

Odee told Derric and Becky about the new calf that was due any time, which opened an opportunity for Derric and Becky to share their news. Walking over to his wife, Derric sat down on the couch and put his arm around her. "We have some news as well," Derric started. "You are going to be grandparents!" Maggie rushed over to hug them both, and Derric reached around his mom and shook his dad's hand. Miah had never seen so much excitement before and couldn't help being a little excited himself. At the same time, he wondered if that would change things for him. Looking over his mom's shoulder, Derric seemed to sense Miah's concern and gave him a friendly wink. The next hour was consumed with dates, ultrasounds, and baby names. Odee even shared a story about how he had gotten his unusual name, making everyone laugh.

Dinner was a happy affair that evening. Odee had placed an extra panel in the kitchen table and added extra chairs for Becky and Derric. They were like one big, happy family, Miah thought to himself. He prayed it would continue. Now that he had experienced being part of a family again, it would be all the harder to have to go back out on his own. He only wished his mother were here to experience it with him. Maggie brought out a scrumptious pineapple upside-down cake for dessert, which was Derric's favorite. After the first bite, Miah could understand exactly why!

The weekend flew by with Derric helping Miah and Odee with chores so they could all play games on Saturday and color Easter eggs. Miah could barely remember coloring eggs before, and he and Derric had a contest to see who could color the darkest egg. Playing games was another first for Miah, but they were all patient with him and he actually won the last game of Trouble as the evening came to an end.

The Easter Sunday service at church was enlightening, and the story of Jesus dying on the cross and rising from death touched Miah's heart. He could hardly believe one man could be willing to die for others' sins. He didn't think he could ever be that brave. It made him want to know more about this amazing man. After the service, everyone came up to say hello to Derric and welcome him and Becky. It was easy for Miah to see that Derric was well liked in the community.

After church, Miah had another surprise. They were going to have an Easter egg hunt. Maggie explained that Odee was out hiding all the colored eggs, and there would be a special prize for the one who found the most. Derric, Becky, and Miah were all ready when Odee came in and said it was time to start. Laughing and running out the door like children, they started the hunt. They had a blast looking in corners, under the woodpile, and around Derric's Jeep. At one point, Miah snatched an egg just as Derric was reaching for it, which caused Maggie, Odee, and even Becky to laugh out loud at the look of disbelief on Derric's face. It was endearing to see Derric help his wife find extra eggs, and it was easy to see that Derric knew all the old hiding places. Still, knowing this, Odee had taken care to hide them in unusual and different places, so it was actually Miah who came out one egg ahead of everyone in the end. He was the winner of the special prize, a giant chocolate rabbit!

After the egg hunt, Derric suggested they go upstairs and look at the computer while the ladies were finishing up dinner. Once upstairs, he looked around fondly at his old room. He pointed out a couple of his favorite books and showed Miah how to set up folders for homework on the computer. He explained a couple of the tools he had placed on the home page and showed Miah how to use them. He noticed that Miah was a good listener and very quick to pick up on the new information. He took a moment to write down his address and phone number and encouraged him to call him and Becky anytime. He told Miah it would be great to have someone at the farm he could call to check on his parents and thanked him again for all the help he was providing. As they left the room to head down for dinner, Miah felt as if he had made a good friend and knew he was going to be as sad as Maggie and Odee when Derric and Becky left.

Chapter 12

With spring came the birth of the calf they had all been expecting, and as with so many births, it came in the middle of the night. Miah was startled at first when Odee came to shake him awake to help with the birth. Miah was so excited that he put his sweatshirt on backwards on his way out the door. They would all laugh about that later.

The birth went well with Odee calming the mama cow and helping her when it came time to push the baby out. He wore long rubber gloves and helped guide the baby out onto the hay at just the right moment. Miah handed him what he needed and actually cut the cord while Odee calmed the excited mama. Miah was amazed when the brand-new baby stood up on wobbly legs and took the first drink of his tired mama's milk. He helped Odee clean up the mess, made easier by the thick plastic Odee had laid under and around the mama beforehand. Miah sat and stared for almost an hour while Odee bustled around putting tools away and placing hay around the stall. The baby was a female and settled happily with her mama once she had finished feeding. It was almost three o'clock in the morning by the time they headed back inside, and Odee declared they would sleep a little later this morning and chores could wait for a bit. Tired after all the excitement, Miah slipped out of his clothes and fell back into bed, asleep almost immediately.

After the excitement of the new calf, things settled down at the farm. There were so many new experiences for Miah that spring and summer. He helped Odee plant a garden and a field of corn that would supply food for the cows. He finally went into town a couple of times with Odee and Maggie, discovering it could be fun and nobody was watching and waiting to snatch him and force him back into foster care. He decided to use some of his earnings to buy a phone. Odee helped him set up a plan that could be added to theirs, agreeing to take the payment out of what Miah earned. Excited, he called Derric first thing and told him about everything going on at the farm. Derric smiled, thinking that Miah was finally getting a little taste of being a regular teenager.

Well into summer, the Hewitts began talking about taking a trip in November to welcome their new grandchild. They discussed dates and were already looking for flights. When Miah mentioned that he could keep things going on the farm, Maggie and Odee both gave him a strange look. "We want you to go with us," they both said, almost in unison.

"Don't you want to see the new baby?" Maggie added in disbelief, already thinking of Miah as part of their family. Unknown to Miah, they were considering officially adopting him, hoping to set his mind at ease about his future. Derric had a close friend who was an attorney, and he was looking into it for them, making sure there would not be repercussions for Miah if the adoption was blocked for some reason. They were hoping to hear from him soon, but, regardless of the outcome, they thought of Miah as part of their family.

"Well, of course I would like to see the baby and Derric and Becky, too," Miah mumbled. "But who will take care of the farm and chores? And what about the extra cost?"

"We have friends and a church family to help us out with that," Odee stated calmly. "Of course, you will come with us, we consider you part of the family now. Not another word about the cost. Derric and Becky will be crushed if we don't bring you along."

Miah couldn't believe his ears. He was choked up a bit about what they were saying and being part of their family. Was he really going to be part of their family forever? He really couldn't comprehend it. Besides, he had never flown—never been anywhere other than Michigan and the surrounding states. San Francisco? Flying in an airplane? He really couldn't even imagine it!

Maggie and Odee went on talking about the trip, the timing, and the coming holidays. The baby was due November 20, so they planned to make it a two-week trip so they could be there for Thanksgiving as well. Miah couldn't wait to tell Derric he was coming with them!

Miah also got to experience camp for the first time that summer. Maggie and Odee had encouraged him to go on the youth camp outing planned for August. It was for a week, so Miah immediately fretted about who would help around the farm, but the Hewitts dismissed it, saying they thought they could manage quite well for a week. Miah had become good friends with some of the youth at their church, especially a boy his age named Carson. He had been to his home a couple of times and really enjoyed spending time with him. They both liked the outdoors and loved music and reading, so they were a good fit. Odee often teased Miah that he liked spending time with Carson because of his cute little sister, Janie, who was only a year younger. Miah always blushed but would not take the bait!

His week at camp was more than he hoped for. He had been reading his Bible and learning all he could, but the time spent in worship with kids his own age had a lasting effect. After talking at one of their worship sessions, Miah made the decision to give his heart to the Lord. He knew that the experience of kneeling, praying, and finally turning his life completely over to God was once in a lifetime. He also knew without a doubt that God had brought him to the Hewitt's farm, and that it was all part of His plan. After the hugs and congratulations from the staff and his friends, Miah called the Hewitts and told them the good news. He could hear the happiness in their voices, and he knew that at least Maggie was crying. Saying he would tell them all about it when he got home, he put his phone away and went back to his friends.

When they picked him up from camp, Odee and Maggie couldn't wait to hear about his experience and his decision to give his heart to the Lord. They told him they were very proud of him and admitted they had a surprise for him as well. They parked in the driveway and walked him out toward the back of the barn. Sitting off to the side was an old car that had obviously been refurbished and newly painted. It wasn't fancy, but they told him it was his if he wanted to learn to drive it. Miah walked over and touched the car, hardly able to believe it was real. He didn't care what kind of car it was, and he couldn't wait to learn to drive it. He kept shaking his head and saying, "A car!" over and over again. Odee told him to hop inside, and he could have his first lesson. Maggie shook her head at the two of them and walked back to get his things out of their car. It was the first of many driving lessons Odee patiently gave Miah at the end of each day's chores. By the end of summer, Miah was ready to go into town and take a driving test. He passed with flying colors on the very first try!

Summer turned into fall, and Miah got to experience the harvest. He picked apples from the apple tree down by the pond, and Maggie made apple hand-pies and canned applesauce. The smells were intoxicating! They worked hard to harvest the field of corn and fill the silo, but Miah didn't mind the work at all. He loved being outside and learning how to manage everything about the farm.

His schooling was also coming along very well, and Maggie was amazed at how quick he was to finish classes. He was a whiz when it came to comprehension and aced most of his exams. He was definitely going to finish early and had already scored extremely high on his pre-SAT test. His writing was exceptional as well, and he needed very little assistance with the program now. Maggie didn't want to concern him by mentioning it, but college was definitely a possibility in his future. He was a very bright young man indeed, and Maggie could tell how much he loved working on his education. She would have to turn this over to God and count on Him to lead Miah on the path He had created him to follow. Only time would tell what the future might hold for someone as talented as this boy. It almost broke her heart to think his gifts had been overlooked by so many others.

Chapter 13

Maggie got a call from Derric in early October with the news they had been waiting for. All they had to do was sign the papers his friend had drawn up and a form from the state of Michigan and send them back. They had already been mailed to the Hewitts. The state was happy to let them adopt Miah since kids his age were rarely adopted. All that was left was to tell him and get his approval. Maggie was so excited, she headed out to find Odee the minute she hung up the phone.

She found Odee in the little office off the milking shed. Hardly able to contain herself, she started in right away, telling Odee about Derric's call and the good news. Odee was thrilled! He jumped right up and hugged her! He had become so attached to Miah he couldn't imagine the farm or family without him. Miah's love of the farm and interest in helping him was something he had not really experienced with Derric. It had brought them close, and he had come to depend on the boy being there. To think he could have another son was more than he had ever hoped for. They decided to ask Miah about it at dinner, and Odee reminded Maggie to go slow. If for some reason the boy did not agree, of course they would respect his wishes. Maybe he wanted things to stay as they were.

That night at dinner, Miah thought the Hewitts must have news from Derric and Becky. They kept looking at him, and he felt that they had something they were dying to tell him. It finally came out as they were eating dessert. Maggie started out by stating the obvious: "Miah, we have something we would like to talk to you about."

"We just want you to consider it, Miah," Odee added seriously. "We aren't pushing you to do it, son."

Now Miah was getting concerned. What on earth were they talking about? Did they want him to leave? A look of panic appeared on his face.

"It's good news," Maggie added quickly, noticing his concern. "At least we think it is. We want to adopt you!"

"Adopt me?" Miah questioned. "I'm sixteen years old. Why would you want to adopt me?" Adoption had never occurred to Miah who had been told time and time again by his caseworkers over the years that adoption wasn't likely. Nobody wanted a ten-year-old child, so he had given up on that idea long ago.

"We want to protect you from ever being questioned about where you belong again, or thinking you aren't welcome, or don't have anyone who cares about you. We want you to belong to our family. We love you." Odee added his comments in a matter of fact tone, but Miah could see tears starting in his eyes. And looking over at Maggie, he could see tears on her face as well even though she was smiling.

Still, Miah was a bit confused. He didn't want to hurt these wonderful people, but he couldn't quite grasp what it all meant. Maggie could see the confusion on the boy's face and wanted to take it away. "Derric has a friend who is an attorney," she explained. "He asked him to look into the possibility, so he reached out to Child Protective Services for the state of Michigan and verified that you are still considered a minor and are eligible for adoption. They sent him a form that we all must sign and the necessary papers for adoption. They should be coming in the mail any day now. But, Miah, it is totally your decision. We would only move forward with it if you agreed. At eighteen, they will consider you an adult, and you will no longer be in their system. And they aren't even likely to search for you if you stay out of Michigan, but if they located you, they could put you with new foster parents. You should also know that Odee and I were licensed at one time as foster parents ourselves in order to take in a friend of Derric's back in the day. We would step up and offer to be reinstated if necessary, but by adopting you, we make you ours forever. That is what we want. A chance to have another son . . . and Derric and Becky are almost as excited as we are!"

Miah looked at Odee and Maggie. There they sat, looking at him earnestly, hoping he would consider letting them adopt him. Were they crazy? Did they really think he would even hesitate to be part of this family forever? But they didn't know everything. Would they still want him to be part of their family if he told them about the baby he abandoned on someone's doorstep? He had to tell them, but seeing the kind faces looking at him lovingly, he just couldn't do it. He told them he needed to think about it and quickly left the room.

Maggie and Odee just looked at each other, and Maggie started crying. Odee went over to provide comfort and told her to give him just a little time; he would come around. But Maggie knew there was something more. She sensed there was something holding Miah back. She just hoped he hadn't done anything that would result in their plans falling apart. She called Derric to tell him what had happened.

Miah headed outside to think. He loved Maggie and Odee, but he didn't want them to be ashamed of him. He had never been able to completely shake the despair he felt at leaving the helpless little baby girl on the doorstep of the girls' home. What if they had mistreated her or simply turned her over to Child Protective Services? He knew how bad that could be. He wanted to be part of their family desperately, but he couldn't accept their offer without telling them the whole truth. And he just couldn't bring himself to do that and ruin the way they felt about him.

He was sitting down by the pond where not too long ago he had been happily picking apples for Maggie. How quickly things could change. Back then, he had been on top of the world. Now he didn't know what he was going to do. Suddenly, the cell phone in his pocket rang, and not even thinking, he answered it. It was Derric. It was obvious he had talked to his parents. He asked Miah if something was bothering him about his parents or staying at the farm. Miah assured them it was nothing to do with them. Derric told Miah how happy he would be to have a brother, which only made Miah feel worse. Derric's kindness was getting to him, and he had never had another person with whom to share things. He was so distraught that before he knew it, he was spilling everything to Derric about Star, the baby, and how he had come to find the farm in the first place. Derric just listened, encouraging Miah to get it all off his chest. When Miah finally finished, there was silence until Derric finally spoke up.

"First, you weren't responsible for that baby," Derric said quietly. "You know that, right?"

"She didn't have anyone else," Miah said sadly. "She only had me. Her mother knew I wouldn't just leave her."

"Yeah, well *she* shouldn't have left her. She had to know you couldn't go to the authorities for fear they would take you back to Michigan. She left you in a no-win situation, Miah."

"I know, I know," Miah answered. "I still feel bad about it all—like I should have done more. I wish I could check on her and see how she is doing. I don't know if I could even find the place again."

"Do you know the name of the place . . . or the name of the town?" Derric questioned.

"The sign on the house said, 'Heavenly Home for Girls.' That's all I remember," Miah answered.

"Well, my best advice is to pray about it and turn it over to God if you can. I will keep this to myself, Miah. But you really should explain all this to mom and dad. I don't think you are going to get the reaction you think you are. I would do a little research on-line and see if you can come up with an address for the school. You could always go by the school and see how she is doing. Would that make you feel better?"

"I think it would," Miah replied. "You are right. I am going to pray about it and see what I can find out about the school. Thank you for calling, Derric, it means the world to me."

"No problem," Derric replied. "I really enjoy having you around, and I hope you will still consider letting my parents adopt you. They don't have to know about the baby first, you know. They love you Miah, and they will understand once you explain the situation. On the other hand, see what you find out, and it can stay between you and me if that makes you feel better. Trust me, Miah, we all have things we would rather our parents know nothing about." Derric said he would talk to him later and encouraged him to give him a call if he discovered anything about the school. Miah thanked him again and said goodbye.

He went back inside and said good night, heading up to his room. Maggie and Odee didn't know what to think. He couldn't look at them. He couldn't face the disappointment he knew he would see on their faces. Maybe it was time to move on, or maybe Derric was right. Feeling a sense of overwhelming sadness at the thought of leaving the farm, he reached for his Bible. Praying for answers was one of the only things he had left. When he opened his Bible, the piece of paper he had found in Derric's Bible slipped out. Miah had borrowed it and kept it in his Bible now, using it often. Looking at the list, he came across the word *despair* and decided to look up those verses. The first verse he came to was in Philippians.

Do not be anxious about anything, but in everything by prayer and supplication, with thanksgiving, let your requests be made known to God. And the peace of God, which surpasses all understanding, will guard your hearts and your minds in Christ Jesus. (Phil. 4:6–7 ESV)

The verses made him feel better already, but he read on.

> We are afflicted in every way, but not crushed; perplexed, but not driven to despair. (2 Cor. 4:8 ESV)

It suddenly occurred to Miah that the answer might be just as simple as Derric had made it seem. He believed in a loving God who understood his every thought and action. God already knew he had taken the baby to the girls' school to ensure her survival, not to abandon her. He had to turn this over to God now and let His plan for the little girl unfold. He could try to find the school and check on her, but ultimately, he needed to continue to pray for God to watch over and protect her as he had prayed the night he left her. Kneeling by his bed, he prayed, "Dear God, thanks for all of the blessings you have provided me. Thanks for the amazing Hewitt family and for leading me to them. Tonight, I ask for protection for the little baby girl I left at the Heavenly Home for Girls. You know my heart, Lord, and only you know the plan you have for her. Please ensure she is happy and well cared for. Please watch over her until she can come to know you and help me find a way to ensure she is happy and loved. Help me to trust that it was you who guided me there and will keep her safe. I know that you gave up your only Son, Jesus, to die for our sins, and I believe all children are precious in your sight. I give this burden to you tonight, Lord, and ask you to lead me on the path you have planned for me. In your Son's precious name, I pray. Amen."

Miah felt as if a weight had been lifted from him, and he knew he was doing the right thing. He got out his computer and started his research. If he could find a way, he would locate the home and check on the little girl. In the meantime, he decided to keep this between him and Derric. And he didn't see any reason why he should not accept Maggie and Odee's offer of adoption. There was no family in the entire world he would rather be a part of. Peeking downstairs, he could see they had already gone to bed. Getting in bed himself, he decided the news would keep until breakfast.

Chapter 14

The next morning, Miah noticed the sun just beginning to rise. He was struck by the beauty, which he took as a sign that God was shining His blessing on Miah's decision and action the night before. He hurried through his morning routine, anxious to share his news with Maggie and Odee.

When he reached the kitchen, he saw them already seated at the table solemnly drinking their coffee. He walked over to Maggie and gave her a hug from behind, repeating the gesture with Odee. Sitting down at the table, with tears in his eyes, he said, "I apologize for the way I acted last night. I think I was just overwhelmed, and I didn't handle it well. I want you both to know there is nothing in the world I would like more than becoming part of your family. The time I have spent with you here has been some of the best time of my life, except for the years with my mom. You have fed me, housed me, and brought me back to Jesus. You have asked for little in return, accepting me for who I am, and trusting me without reason. I know, without a doubt, my mom would love you. You have an extraordinary family, and it would be an honor to join it."

It was absolutely quiet for just an instant, and then everyone started talking at once. They all looked at each other and started laughing. "Well that settles it then, son." Odee looked at Maggie and said proudly, "I guess we have ourselves another boy!"

"We have to call Derric and Becky," Maggie said with excitement. I know they are waiting to hear. She got her cell phone and dialed the number. "Derric," she said seriously when he answered. "You have a brother!" Miah and Odee smiled as they heard a loud, "Woo hoo!" coming over the phone.

A few days later, the papers arrived in the mail, and they went through them carefully, finally signing their names in the appropriate places. They made copies and carefully placed everything required back in the big manila envelope. Now all they had to do was to wait for the certificate of adoption that would make Miah an official member of the Hewitt family.

In the meantime, they were getting things around for their trip to San Francisco. With some of his earnings, Miah had purchased a couple of new shirts and a pair of jeans along with a sturdy duffle bag. He carefully placed what he would need for the trip in the bag. Maggie had gotten him new sneakers the last time they were in town when she noticed him looking at a pair in the sporting goods store. She told him he could consider them an early Christmas present. Looking down at them now, he was happy that he would look better when they went to visit Derric and Becky. He could hardly wait to see some of the things Derric had told him recently on the phone. And Derric said he might have some information on the baby girl Miah had left at the home by the time they arrived. Miah felt like the burden had lifted a little since he had shared the truth with Derric, but he still hadn't told Maggie and Odee.

When they arrived in San Francisco, the weather was sunny and beautiful. Derric met them at the airport, but Becky was too uncomfortable to travel and had opted to wait for them at home. Derric planned to pick up pizza on the way back. They lived in Woodland, a small community on the outskirts of the city. Becky was standing at the window watching for them when they arrived. After hugging her in-laws and Miah, she told Derric that he could put the pizzas in the oven to warm, and they would eat at the table where she had plates and napkins all ready for them. Derric showed his parents to the spare bedroom and told Miah they had put a rollaway bed in the nursery for him. When he asked about the baby coming any minute, Becky reassured him. The baby would sleep in a small bassinet in their room for the first couple of months.

As Miah carried his things into the nursery, he looked around and thought this was one lucky baby! Soft yellow walls had pictures of baby animals in white frames. There was a changing table and dresser in white to match the crib, and a white rocking chair stood in the corner. It was a beautiful room, fit for a queen. They would love this baby girl without question, and Miah couldn't help but think of the other baby girl he had left at the home for girls. He had done a little research and discovered the address of the place he had left her. As he was looking around and studying an ultrasound picture of the baby, Derric walked into the room.

"Let me move that rocking chair into our bedroom and give you a little more room," he commented. "We are hoping to use it soon!" With a wink and a smile, he carried the white rocking chair out of the room. The new rollaway bed looked out of place in the nursery, but it was covered with clean sheets, a soft blanket, and topped with a colorful comforter; it certainly looked comfortable to Miah. He tucked his bag under the bed and headed back to the living room. He wanted to talk to Derric about his research, but he was hungry and tired from his long flight, and the pizza Derric had picked up smelled delicious. It could wait for now.

They all chatted and laughed as they ate their pizza, happy to be back together as a family. Miah could see the love they had for each other and was happy to be part of it. He didn't know how all this had happened after years of dreaming about it, but he was pretty sure now that God had a hand in it. After the meal, they all decided to watch a movie so Becky could lie on the couch. She had been uncomfortable all evening, and Miah felt bad for her, noticing how difficult her movements seemed. He smiled as Derric helped her get situated on the couch, bringing in a pillow from the bedroom and tucking a soft throw over her. He slid down next to Miah on the floor, leaning against the couch to keep an eye on her. She dozed as they all watched a movie called *The Blind Side*, and Miah could certainly relate since the family in the movie adopted a kid off the street who had no real home. Toward the end of the movie, he glanced over at Odee who sat straight up in his chair fast asleep. As they turned off the television and headed to bed, Miah thought he was one lucky guy to be part of this family.

Around five o'clock the next morning, Miah heard a bunch of commotion, jumped out of bed, and peeked out the door just as Maggie was heading to the spare room. She was already dressed and had been in the bathroom brushing her teeth.

"Hurry, get dressed," she told Miah. "It's time to get Becky to the hospital to have the baby."

Flustered a bit, Miah ran back in the nursery and quickly changed out of his pajamas. He grabbed his toothbrush and just had time to use the restroom and brush his teeth before they were all hurrying out to Derric's vehicle. Becky was already in the front seat, and Miah thought it was odd that she was panting a bit like a dog. He saw Odee helping Maggie into the back seat and quickly squeezed in beside her. He smiled to himself when he noticed that she was still holding her toothbrush.

The hospital was just around the corner from them, so they were there in no time. Derric rushed into the emergency entrance and came back out quickly with a nurse and wheelchair. They helped Becky into the hospital as Odee climbed up front and drove the car to the parking lot. They got out and hurried into the hospital where Odee asked for directions to the maternity ward. Within minutes, the three of them were sitting in a small waiting room where Maggie began nervously pacing back and forth. About thirty minutes later, Derric came into the waiting room to tell them everything was fine. Becky's labor was going quickly, but it would still be a while. He suggested they go down to the cafeteria and get some breakfast.

They all trudged down to the cafeteria, but no one was very hungry. They settled on steaming cups of hot chocolate and hurried back to the waiting room. Two hours later, Miah awoke to the sound of Derric exclaiming, "It's a girl!" Soon they were ushered back to a room where Becky sat in bed looking tired but happy. In her arms was a little pink bundle. Pulling the blanket away from the baby's face, she showed the Hewitts their first grandchild.

"We are calling her Hannah Elizabeth," she announced. Maggie beamed as she looked at her and Becky continued. "She will share her grandma's middle name. What do you think Uncle Miah?"

Miah walked over and looked down at the tiny little baby. He touched her hand and was surprised when her little fingers automatically wrapped around one of his. "She's beautiful," was all he could manage to say.

The rest of their time in San Francisco went by in a flash. After getting the baby home and helping Derric and Becky get through the first week of being new parents, they only had time to visit a couple of the places Derric had mentioned to Miah. One night after everyone else had gone to bed, Derric was able to share what he had learned about the baby girl Miah had left at the home for girls. He explained that the home had only been around for about five years and was run by a woman named Mrs. Harper. Unfortunately, the woman was in a terrible accident some time back and had only recently returned to the school. However, a local church had taken an interest in the school and the girls who lived there and had been caring for them in her absence. According to his friend's sources, the school had gotten much better over the past couple of months. Mrs. Harper was very different after her accident and had taken a renewed interest in the girls. There was mention of a baby who had been left on the doorstep, but no one knew her name or circumstances.

"I'm sorry, Miah," Derric concluded. "That's all I really know. You could go back and check on her and make sure she is okay, but it sounds like she is probably fine." Miah nodded and decided to let it go for now. Right after Christmas, he was planning to help out at a church he thought was in the vicinity of the home for girls. It was part of an outreach program of their home church, and he had jumped at the chance to get back that way and relocate the home for girls. If he had time, he would try to visit the home and see what he could find out about the little girl. He prayed they were taking good care of her.

Since Becky and Derric were planning to visit Becky's family over Christmas, the Hewitts had suggested having Christmas before they returned home. Maggie, Odee, and Miah had gone shopping while Becky was still in the hospital, and the presents were wrapped and waiting. The day before they left, Maggie prepared a wonderful Christmas dinner with a huge ham and all the trimmings. Miah and Derric even helped her decorate Christmas cookies! After dinner, they handed out presents, and Miah couldn't wait to give Derric and

Becky the soft, warm throw he had picked out for them and a tiny sleeper for the new baby. Derric and Becky surprised him in return with a new backpack full of school supplies and the latest/greatest calculator, which would be a big help with his schoolwork. He could finally get rid of the ragged backpack that he had carried for years.

Miah saw how happy Maggie and Odee were. He watched them with their tiny granddaughter and shared in their awe at how perfect she was. He joined in with their laughter when Odee opened the giant remote Derric gave him as a gag gift. (Odee was always losing the television remote.) When he finally held his niece by himself for the very first time, he was amazed at how proud he felt.

The next day was a flurry of packing and getting ready to return home. They hugged Becky and the baby saying their final goodbyes and headed out to the car. Derric took them to the airport, and gave Miah a hug and reminded him that he was always welcome to visit. As he boarded the plane with Odee and Maggie at his side, Miah could not remember ever feeling like part of such a big, happy family!

Chapter 15

December was a busy month at the farm with the extra work of chopping more wood and making sure the animals were warm and dry in the barn when the inevitable snow and ice visited. Miah wrapped up his on-line classes in preparation for the winter break and was extremely pleased when all his exams came back with perfect scores! Maggie made his favorite cookies to celebrate, and Miah felt like he had finally made up for all the education he had missed over the years.

Christmas was an awesome experience for Miah even though he had gotten to experience a bit of it in San Francisco. There was the whole experience of tromping out to the woods to find just the right pine tree to suit Maggie, then chopping it down and dragging it through the snow and onto the porch. They shook off all the loose snow and needles before bringing it inside and putting it in a stand ready for decorations. They strung ornaments for hours, and Maggie had to share each one's story with Miah before hanging it on the tree. When all the ornaments had been hung, Maggie handed Miah a small package. When he opened it questioningly, he found a tiny manger with the baby Jesus lying in the center.

"To remind you of the year you accepted Christ," Maggie said proudly. Miah hugged her and placed his ornament on the tree.

That night after supper, Maggie popped a big bowl of popcorn, and the three of them sat at the table stringing it on thread and then placing it on the Christmas tree. Miah thought it was about the most beautiful tree he had ever seen with all the ornaments, lights, and the fluffy, white popcorn.

One afternoon, Miah begged off chores early wanting to go into town to do a bit of Christmas shopping.

He parked his car carefully in front of the department store and went inside. He needed to find Maggie and Odee something special for Christmas. As he was walking around and looking at some warm, comfy-looking slippers for Maggie, a sales clerk came up and asked him if she could help. Looking up, he noticed it was Janie, his friend Carson's sister. She really was a cute girl, and he almost stammered when he said hello, afraid she might know what he was thinking. Janie turned out to be very helpful, showing Miah a soft, flannel nightgown that matched the slippers he had been looking at. He knew Maggie would love them! When Janie asked him if there was anything else, he told her that he was thinking about a new flannel shirt for Odee. She took him over to the men's department where there were several rows of soft, flannel shirts. As they were looking through them, they both reached for one at the same moment. Their hands touched as they both chose a deep-burgundy and gray shirt, and Miah quickly decided it was the one for Odee. (Even if it was purple with green elephants on it, he would have purchased it just because she liked it, he thought to himself with a smile.) Janie showed Miah some warm winter socks for Odee as well, and Miah's shopping was done. He waited when she offered to gift-wrap them and thanked her several times. Finally, he made his way back to the car, noticing that Janie was still watching him from the store window as he drove away.

On Christmas Eve, Maggie kept suggesting that Miah hang a stocking on the mantle. Miah finally gave in, telling her it was silly but feeling like a kid at the same time. That night as he lay in bed before drifting off to sleep, he remembered a time with his mom when he had hung a stocking next to their Christmas tree and even left cookies and milk for Santa. The memories warmed his heart, and for once, thinking about his mom did not bring on the rush of sadness it usually did.

The next morning, he was surprised to see that his stocking was bursting at the seams! There were all kinds of goodies in the stocking including candy, a hair comb, toothbrush and toothpaste, socks, a mystery novel, and a brand-new jackknife at the very bottom. He noticed with a smile that it was very similar to the one he had admired Odee using one day.

Once he had emptied his stocking, he picked up the packages for Odee and Maggie he had placed under the tree. Maggie and Odee loved their presents. Odee put on the flannel shirt, and Miah laughed as he buttoned it right over his pajamas commenting on how soft it was. Maggie put on her new slippers and told him they were perfect! They told Miah it was his turn and sent him after the other presents under the tree. Odee and Maggie had already opened their gifts from one another, so the rest of the gifts were for Miah. Miah had grown almost a foot since he had been at the farm, so many of his things were getting too small. He opened the packages, thrilled to get a winter coat, jeans, two shirts, and a pair of hiking boots he had been admiring. Odee, ever the more practical of the two, had gotten him jumper cables for his car, which had been having a little trouble starting now and then in the cold weather. Miah hugged both of them, thinking there wasn't a better place in the entire world God could have taken him than this little farm in Ohio.

Maggie had made giant pecan rolls for breakfast along with crisp bacon and fresh-squeezed orange juice. They finally went upstairs and got dressed, laughing at the length of time they had all stayed in their pajamas. Later, they played cards and a game of Yatzee while dinner was in the oven. Then they all pigged-out on the tasty roast beef dinner Maggie had prepared, knowing it was one of their favorites.

After dinner, Miah restocked the woodbin and helped Odee check on the animals and finish chores. He saw the calico kitten up in the loft and stopped to pet her and make sure her and her mama had food and water. The rest of the litter had found homes, but Odee had kept the little calico around knowing Miah was partial to her. He was thrilled and had named her Callie since he had always called her the little calico. As they finished the chores and headed inside, Odee put his arm around Miah's shoulders giving him a quick hug.

"You are such a blessing to us, Miah," he said. "This has been a wonderful Christmas!" They went inside and hung up their coats just in time for a piece of Maggie's delicious coconut cream pie. Miah was so stuffed he thought he would burst. Gone was the skinny, toothpick of a boy who had shown up at their door almost a year earlier. No one would even guess it was the same person today. They all sat by the fire working on a Christmas puzzle Maggie had started earlier in the week, finishing it just before bedtime. Just before they headed upstairs, Odee got out his Bible and read the Christmas story. Before he drifted off to sleep that night, Miah remembered thinking, "Best Christmas ever!"

Chapter 16

Right after Christmas, it was time to head off with his friends from church to work on the outreach program they had planned. They would be staying at the church's outreach center for the homeless through New Year's Eve. Miah thought he could really help with this program, having been homeless himself. He also had written down the address for the Heavenly Home for Girls where he had left the baby almost a year ago. He was keeping it to himself and secretly hoped to pay the school a visit while he was in the area.

The program was a huge success, but Miah was anxious about getting to the girls' home. Finally, on the last night before their time at the shelter ended, he found a couple of hours in the evening when he could slip away. Driving the old car Odee had given him, he made his way to the neighborhood, parking one street over from where the home was located. He went to the door but just couldn't find the courage to knock. Instead, he made his way over to the first-floor windows, and, staying in the shadows, he stood watching the girls. As he stood there, he realized it was New Year's Eve. He could hear their laughter and see them all hugging, singing, and saying something about being sisters. Finally, he heard one of the ladies say, "Welcome to the Harper family." Just as it dawned on him that she was making them all a part of her family, he saw her look toward the window. Ducking down, he held his breath. When nothing happened, he left the window and quickly made his way back to his car, thanking God for once again answering his prayers. As he drove back to the outreach center, he realized something else. His mom had been right when she told him, "God is with us, and there is always hope."

He was almost back to the shelter when he heard a loud bang, and the car jerked to one side. He was able to bring it to a stop, but he was shaking when he finally stepped out of the car. Walking around to the rear, he saw that he had blown a tire. Relieved that it was only a flat tire, he opened the trunk to pull out his spare, thankful that Odee had taken the time to show him how to change it. He had finished putting on the spare tire and was putting his flat in the trunk when he felt a blow to his head, and everything went black.

When Miah finally came to, his car was gone and his head was throbbing! Someone had come up behind him, knocked him out, and stolen his car! When he reached up to gently explore his throbbing head, his hand came back covered in blood! He was hurt badly and had no way to get back to the shelter.

They were supposed to leave for home in the morning, and he hadn't told anyone where he was going. He shivered in the cold, knowing he had to think of something! Suddenly, he realized his cell phone was in his pocket. He could call for help. He looked up his friend's number and dialed nervously. He hated having to admit what had happened. Carson was concerned and said he was heading his way worried at the shaky sound of his friend's voice on the phone.

About ten minutes later, Miah saw a car coming slowly down the road. His mouth went dry as the thought occurred to him that whoever took his car might be coming back. He tried to get up, but everything started spinning, and he quickly sat back down, groaning as the movement shot a stab of pain in his head. As the car stopped, he recognized Carson and one of his chaperones from church getting out. Sighing in relief, he waited for them. They helped Miah as he stood up shakily, telling them he didn't feel too well. His hand was covered in blood from holding his head, and Carson could see that the wound was still seeping. Their chaperone, Mr. VanVleet, took one look and immediately determined that it was necessary to take Miah to the nearby hospital to be checked out. Miah was in too much pain to resist.

When they got to the hospital, Mr. VanVleet explained what had happened, and they took Miah back immediately to check the wound. Once they had cleaned it up and given him a shot for the pain, a doctor came in to explain that he was going to need some stitches in the back of his head. He had been hit with a blunt object, and they had already called the police to come in and take a statement from Miah about what had happened. In the meantime, they were going to take good care of him.

The police were kind but thorough, asking Miah a lot of questions about the incident. They told him they would be looking into it. Miah gave them directions to where he thought it had happened, starting to feel drowsy from the medication and the whole ordeal.

Finally, they were released to head back to the shelter. It had taken hours at the hospital and Miah was exhausted. However, when Mr. VanVleet mentioned he had contacted the Hewitts, Miah sat up sharply and groaned with pain and anxiety.

"I'm sorry, son, but we had to let them know, and the hospital had to get their permission to treat you. You must know how serious this is, Miah, and I have to say I am disappointed that you left the shelter without letting anyone know what you were doing. This situation could have been much worse."

"I'm sorry, sir," was all Miah could manage.

As they pulled into the parking lot at the shelter, Odee and Maggie rushed out to greet them. Once they were convinced that Miah was going to be okay, they agreed to let him get some rest, and they would head home in the morning. It was late by now, and they had already driven all the way from the farm. Miah sat down on one of the sofas and kept saying he was sorry. Everyone could see how shaken he was. Mr. VanVleet brought him a pillow and blanket and suggested he stay on the couch where someone could monitor him. They kept reminding him that he could not have done anything differently. Eventually the drugs took effect, and Miah drifted off to sleep. Maggie and Odee stayed with him, using the other sofa to take turns getting a couple hours of sleep. They had to wake him every couple of hours to make sure he was okay.

The next morning, the police visited the shelter and informed Miah they had found his tire iron along the side of the road near where the incident had happened. They were in the process of checking it for fingerprints and hoped to use the results to help them track down the people responsible. They would notify Miah and the Hewitts if they were able to identify suspects and would continue to search for Miah's vehicle. Miah listened to everything through the pounding pain in his head, wanting nothing more than to be back at the farm in his own room.

When they got back home, Miah spent almost a week in his room. He insisted on coming downstairs for meals, and Odee told Maggie to quit fussing over him. Maggie took him to get the stitches out, and the doctor declared him well enough to go back to normal activities. He still felt somewhat embarrassed about the whole incident. They had all talked when they returned to the farm, and Miah had finally confessed to dropping off the baby at the Heavenly Home for Girls. He explained that he had discovered the address on the computer and wanted to make sure she was okay. While Maggie and Odee understood his reason for going there, they let Miah know that going alone and not getting permission to leave the church group that night was definitely the wrong thing to do. It could have been so much worse, and they were all thankful that Miah had his cell phone on him that night. Miah agreed and apologized again, assuring them he would not make the same mistake in the future. He was relieved to have shared the burden of the baby with the Hewitts and happy to know that they didn't feel differently about him as a result. In fact, they suggested going with him the next time if he wanted to visit her.

Almost a month later, Miah was finally able to put the incident behind him for good. The police notified him that his car had been recovered, but was in very bad shape. Unfortunately, they had not been able to identify those responsible from the partial fingerprints discovered on the tire iron. Odee and Miah made the trip back to inspect the vehicle. After getting someone to provide documentation that the vehicle was beyond repair, they decided to use any funds their insurance provided toward the purchase of another vehicle. It had been a costly lesson learned, and Miah was glad it was finally over.

Chapter 17

In June, Miah graduated from his on-line high school with high honors. He had turned seventeen in January and had done an outstanding job with his studies. He had received a letter in the mail shortly afterward congratulating him on maintaining the highest grade-point average of the entire on-line class of students who were all older than he was; there were over three hundred students in his class! The letter invited him to a ceremony at the local college where they would like him to be their guest of honor along with a couple of other students. Maggie and Odee were thrilled and told Miah they would be proud to accompany him.

The night of the ceremony Miah got ready upstairs, putting on a shirt and tie Maggie was adamant about buying him, along with new khaki pants. He wore a pair of loafers Derric had left in his closet that fit him perfectly! As he came downstairs to ask Odee to help with his tie, he saw Maggie beaming at him. He smiled back nervously never having experienced anything quite like this and thankful that she and Odee would be there with him. He heard a knock on the door and gave Maggie a questioning look as Odee answered the door. The next thing he knew Derric and Becky came rushing into the room with little Hannah in Becky's arms.

Derric came over and gave Miah a bear hug. "You didn't think we would miss your graduation, did you, bro?"

"We are so proud of you," Becky added. She handed Hannah to Derric and gave Miah a hug of her own.

"You came all the way from San Francisco for my graduation," Miah said. "That's *crazy!*"

"You're the only brother we have," Derric said. "We wouldn't miss it for the world!"

"Okay, okay," Odee told them as he ushered them toward the door. "Let's go, or we are going to be late!"

When they arrived at the college and went inside, there was a gentleman waiting to seat Miah up on the podium with four other students. Once Miah was seated, the gentleman led his family to the front row in the audience.

My family, Miah thought to himself as they were seated. *I have a real family!*

There was a guest speaker who talked about academic excellence and its importance. After his speech, he announced that each of the students seated on the stage had worked tirelessly to finish high school independently and had been chosen to receive scholarships for academic excellence. The first two students received twenty-thousand-dollar scholarships to a college of their choice, and the next two received thirty-thousand-dollar scholarships. Miah was the last student to be called. After announcing to everyone that Miah had achieved the highest grade-point of over three hundred students in spite of being the youngest member of his class, applause erupted from the audience. Once the audience quieted, the speaker announced that Miah would receive a two-year, all-expenses-paid scholarship to the college of his choice, and would be eligible for an additional scholarship if he continued to achieve academic excellence after the first two years. Maggie and Odee were invited to the stage to congratulate him. Miah was embarrassed by all the attention but proud of what he had accomplished and happy he was now assured a college education. All the hard work and late nights had definitely paid off.

After the ceremony, the Hewitts all went to a nearby restaurant to celebrate. Miah was so happy to see Derric, Becky, and his cute little niece. He basked in their praise and shared what had been going on since their last visit, leaving out the incident at the Heavenly Home for Girls. He would tell Derric about that later. They had a wonderful meal and headed home where they all put on comfortable clothes and sat around talking until after midnight!

Derric and Becky stayed for a week. Miah showed Derric a new spreadsheet he had developed to help Odee with the accounting for the farm, and Derric was impressed with his abilities on the computer. They took a walk around the farm one evening after chores, and Miah shared his story about his visit to the home for girls and his resulting accident. Derric was happy it had all turned out okay, but he added his own warnings about handling it better in the future. Miah was embarrassed, but at the same time, he was happy to have a big brother to talk to about it. They also discussed his options for college, and Derric was surprised, but happy, that one of the options Miah was considering involved staying at the farm.

When Derric and Becky got ready to leave, they handed Miah a card. Miah noted the excited look Derric exchanged with his parents as he opened the card. As he read the front of the card, he could feel something inside. Opening it, he found an airline ticket to San Francisco for the first week in July.

Derric couldn't stand it any longer. "We want you to visit us for a couple of weeks before you start college," he said. "I can show you around, take you where I work, and you can get re-acquainted with your niece."

"Please come," Becky added.

Miah didn't know what to say. He finally looked at Odee and questioned, "What about the farm and chores?"

"I can get someone to help while you are gone, son," he stated. "You have earned a vacation. Go have some fun!"

Miah pulled Derric and Becky in for a group hug including baby Hannah. "Okay, I'd love to come. Thank you, guys, so much!"

Knowing he would be seeing them all in a few weeks made saying goodbye a lot easier. As they pulled out of the driveway and Maggie and Odee stood with him watching them leave, Miah stood silently praying and thanking God for these wonderful people.

Chapter 18

Miah's trip to San Francisco was unforgettable! Derric and Becky showed him around the city, and Derric took him to his workplace where it was obvious that Derric was highly regarded. Miah was surprised by the pride he felt in seeing Derric in this light. He knew without a doubt that they had truly become brothers in the past year and a half.

One day, Derric got called into work to assist with a computer glitch, and Miah offered to spend the day watching his niece so Becky could run a couple of errands. He marveled at how much he enjoyed playing with the baby girl and couldn't help but feel a bit nostalgic about the other baby girl in his past. He pushed it out of his mind, knowing that she was in a good environment, while he thoroughly enjoyed spending time with his tiny niece. He was adept at changing her and feeding her, and when Becky walked in, she found him tickling Hannah as she lay on a blanket on the floor. The baby was laughing out loud, and Becky could see that Miah was completely at ease with her. It made her happy to know that her baby girl had a wonderful uncle like Miah.

All too soon, Miah's time in San Francisco came to an end. He thanked Derric and Becky, kissed little Hannah goodbye, and enjoyed the short ride back to the airport with Derric where he shared his plans for college. Derric listened intently and thanked Miah for all he was doing for their parents. He knew how much they meant to Miah; it was obvious as he explained his plans for the future. He also knew that Miah's involvement in the farm meant the world to their parents, especially Odee. He was thankful to have Miah in their lives, all their lives. At the airport, he gave his brother a hug, letting him know that he was loved and welcome to visit any time. Still, as much as Miah had enjoyed his time in San Francisco, he had missed Maggie and Odee a lot. Sitting on the plane, he fidgeted with excitement. He could hardly wait to get home!

Miah had decided to stay at the farm and use his scholarship at the local community college, which offered wonderful programs in both business and journalism and even a program in agricultural studies. He planned to do at least two years there before deciding what he wanted to get a four-year degree in. He was leaning toward a business degree, which he figured could help with many things, but he still loved writing, so even journalism was a possibility. He also planned to use some of his electives to get more education in agriculture. He could hardly believe he would be starting college in September. He just hoped his scholarship truly covered expenses so he wouldn't be a burden on the Hewitts, although they had already offered to pay anything that might not be covered. He hoped that the recent news he had received would also help.

In addition to information about the scholarship, they received additional news that was going to make a big difference in Miah's future. His mother had invested the money she had received from the Army upon his father's death, and it had been growing all these years. The investment would mature on Miah's eighteenth birthday, and he would have some decisions to make about what to do with it. The Hewitts hoped he would keep it invested and growing at least until he really needed it. With the scholarship Miah had received and the fact that he was starting out at the nearby community college, they would not have a lot of expense for his education. They had intended to take care of that for him anyway since he continued to take on more and more responsibility for the farm. But they also knew that Miah wanted to be independent, and for once in his life, he had the ability to do so.

Chapter 19

The rest of the summer went by quickly. Miah and Maggie went into town to pick up the things Miah would need for school, and Maggie surprised Miah with a brand-new laptop! It was a graduation present from her and Odee, and they told him it was long over-due. Miah was thrilled and spent time getting it all set up and ready for his college classes. He called Derric to tell him all about it, discovering that Derric had been instrumental in helping the Hewitts pick it out. He explained some of the features Miah had questions about, admitting that he had a very similar laptop himself.

The first semester of college flew by with Miah still suggesting that he help with chores before and after classes. He was thrilled to discover that Carson was also enrolled at the community college and was in two of his classes. Since Carson and his sister Janie shared a vehicle, this was also an opportunity for him to get to see Janie occasionally when she dropped her brother off or picked him up. Miah was getting more and more confident talking to her and was even thinking about inviting her out for a movie or dinner.

He got his first chance one day when he came out of his English class to find her waiting in the student lounge for her brother. He invited her to sit down and have something to drink while she waited, quickly getting them drinks from a nearby soda machine. After asking her about how her senior year was going, he brought up an interesting movie he wanted to see. Smiling, she admitted she would enjoy seeing it as well, so he asked her to go with him. As Carson walked up looking at them oddly, Miah felt pretty happy with himself. He had just asked a girl out on his first real date!

Miah and Janie had a great time at the movies, and before long, they were planning things together regularly. Janie had come to dinner at the Hewitts, and both Maggie and Odee thought she was very sweet. Miah had also visited Janie's family, although he was already familiar with them and their home since he had visited Carson often over the past couple of years. Miah was doing well in his classes and was having a blast doing things with Janie. Life was great!

As the holidays approached, Miah decided he wanted to plan a special trip with Janie to do some Christmas shopping. There was a new shopping complex a couple of hours away where they would have a great selection of stores and eateries. After talking with Janie, he got permission from her parents and the Hewitts to make the trip the first Saturday in December. They could celebrate the end of his first semester of college at the same time since his Christmas break started the next week. Odee insisted they take his new truck, so they wouldn't have to worry about car problems. Miah was still driving an old car he had purchased with the insurance money from his first car after the accident near the girls' school almost a year ago. Unknown to the Hewitts, he was planning to get some kind of new vehicle with some of the money he would inherit on his birthday in January, but so far, he had not discussed it out in the open. He would discuss it with them after the holidays. He was happy to borrow Odee's truck for the shopping trip.

Miah had been saving most of his earnings from his job at the farm, so he had plenty of money for Christmas this year. It felt good to have the means to buy people what he wanted and not have to worry about every cent. He had become accustomed to having a nice place to live, plenty to eat, and a real family to share life with. His memories of foster care and life on the run had all but faded. He thought often of his mother's words about God and hope, always somewhat astonished by the fact that she had been absolutely right! He said his prayers nightly and was ever grateful for all he had. Now it was he who told people not to forget God was there to watch over them, and there was always hope. His would make sure his mother and her beliefs lived on in him.

The shopping trip with Janie was a huge success. They had fun picking out gifts for Maggie, Odee,

Derric, and Becky. They even took time to find just the right gift for baby Hannah, eventually choosing a huge stuffed teddy bear and a little outfit in a soft, pretty blue to match her eyes. Janie bought gifts for her parents and her brother as well.

Miah kept watching Janie to get some ideas about a gift for her. When she stopped to admire a pretty silver charm bracelet, Miah knew he was going to get it for her. He made up an excuse to go to the truck for something, leaving her at the bookstore to browse. He quickly made his way back to the jewelry store, purchased the bracelet and the charms he wanted, and had the whole thing gift-wrapped. Putting it in one of his other bags, he made his way back to the bookstore. Janie pointed out a book she was interested in, and Miah was happy to get it for her. Janie never suspected he had just purchased her Christmas gift a few minutes before.

With their shopping completed, they started talking about a place to eat. Finally settling on a nearby steakhouse, they headed out to the truck. Suddenly, Miah felt the hairs on the back of his neck start to prickle and glancing back, he saw a man following them. Quickly getting Janie and their packages into the truck, he closed the doors and told her to lock them. Startled, Janie did as she was told, craning her neck to see who was walking up to Miah.

The man was average height and a bit on the stocky size. He had greasy, dark hair and a thin mustache. She was a bit surprised to hear him call Miah "Jerry" and didn't like the tone of the man's voice when he addressed Miah. He was angry, belligerent, and obviously wanted to hurt Miah. More than a little scared, she got out her phone ready to dial 911 if necessary.

Chapter 20

As the man approached, Miah knew almost immediately who it was. His worst nightmare was realized the minute he spoke, and his attitude toward him hadn't changed a bit in over four years.

"Jerry," he sneered. "What do you think you're up to, kid?"

Miah hesitated, trying not to show his fear of the man who had abused him time and time again. Still, he stood his ground, not willing to give in to the fear he still felt around this man. "I don't know that it is any of your business," he replied. "You need to leave."

The man instantly grabbed his arm, jerking him so hard he almost fell over. "Don't you tell me what to do, you rotten no-good kid," he spat. "You're coming with me!"

Miah was a lot stronger now, and he knew how to handle himself. Jerking his arm away from the man, he stood closer to the truck. "You need to leave me alone right now, or I am calling the police," he told him. "You have no say over me now," he said firmly and loudly.

"Oh, just look at the little boy talk," the man sneered. "Is this your truck?" Looking over the truck, he noticed how nice it was and saw Janie sitting in the passenger seat. "Oh, got you a girl, too, huh?" He tried the door, intending to scare Janie, which worked very well. Unknown to him, Janie had called 911 the minute she saw the man grab Miah's arm.

"Get away from her you jerk," Miah told him.

Coming back around to Miah, the man shoved him to the ground, giving him a sharp kick in the side. "Shut up, kid," he snarled. "You're going to pay for talking to me like that! You always were trouble, and I'm going to make sure everybody knows it." He grabbed Miah by the hair, forcing him back to a standing position. Just about the time he started forward to punch him again, someone reached in and grabbed his arm. The man was forced to release his hold on Miah and found himself swung around to face a crowd of people and a police officer.

"What's going on here?" the police officer stated.

"This punk is starting trouble," the man started, in spite of the crowd booing and shouting that he was lying. "He's my foster kid, and he won't do what he's told," the man continued, ignoring the crowd. The officer looked a Miah.

"Is that true?" he asked Miah.

"No sir," Miah responded. "That was years ago, and I have a new family now and have been there for almost two years. I was here shopping with a friend, and he followed us and started this whole thing." Miah got out his license and showed the police officer. "We were just doing some Christmas shopping, and this man followed us to our vehicle." The crowd of people gathered obviously agreed with Miah. One man shouted out that Miah was right; the man started the whole thing.

As the man turned to Miah and started yelling names at him, the police officer got out handcuffs and quickly had him immobilized. "You're coming with us, mister," he said. Turning to Miah, he asked if he would like to press charges.

"No sir," Miah said to the police officer. "We just want him to leave us alone."

"No worries there," the police officer replied. "I believe a night in jail will cool him down. It's obvious he's been drinking. You kids are free to leave. Your girlfriend did the right thing calling 911. Have a good evening." Leading the man away, he pushed him into the back seat of the police car. As it drove away, Miah's nerves kicked in, and he shakily got into the truck when he heard Janie unlock it. All he wanted was to get home as soon as possible.

Miah and Janie picked up some fast food on the way home not wanting to stop anywhere. Miah explained a bit of his past to Janie as they drove, and he was comforted when she reached over and held his hand for the rest of the way home. They called Janie's parents and asked them to meet them at the Hewitts. Miah called Odee, explaining briefly what had happened and letting him know that Janie's parents were coming over.

When they got to the Hewitts, everyone was anxiously waiting for them. After hugs and a quick check of Miah's ribs, which were already turning purple, they all sat down to hear what had happened. Miah was still a bit shaken because the man had brought back many horrible memories. Janie explained part of it and Miah filled in the background now and then. Odee and Maggie listened in disbelief, hearing one more layer of Miah's disturbing foster experience and knowing in their hearts that it never should have been that way. Janie's parents praised them both and thanked Miah for protecting their daughter. All agreed that Miah would go to the doctor the next day to get his ribs checked out. As Janie and her parents drove away, Miah looked up at the Hewitts, and tears came from nowhere and trickled down his face. They gathered the young man into their arms and told him over and over that everything was going to be alright. And for once in his life, he knew it really was.

Miah went to the doctor the next day. The diagnosis was that a couple of his ribs were badly bruised, but nothing was cracked or broken. He should be good as new within a few weeks. Odee tried to keep him from doing chores, but Miah couldn't sit still doing nothing. Janie came over and tried to distract him with her new book and some games, but he was moody and out of sorts. After looking through his books for next semester's classes for a couple of days and wrapping up the rest of his Christmas presents, he was right back outside trying to help with the chores. Ten days later when they went out to cut down a Christmas tree, Miah insisted on going with them and helping to drag it back to the farm, assuring them all that he was as good as new.

Chapter 21

Christmas was another wonderful experience for Miah this year. Derric, Becky, and little Hannah came home for the holidays, and Miah had Janie over as well. Janie was a big hit with little Hannah, who was toddling around enchanting everyone. After Hannah went to bed, they all played cards and made popcorn, enjoying all the special treats Maggie always made during the holidays. Afterward, Miah took Janie home. They made plans to get together the following evening.

On Christmas morning, they exchanged gifts, and everyone declared they had gotten just what they wanted. Miah laughed when little Hannah tried to carry her stuffed bear, which was bigger than she was, everywhere she went.

Later in the evening, Miah made the trip to Janie's house to give her the present he had gotten her. She loved the charm bracelet and the charms he had chosen: a small silver book and a cross. He was surprised at his own gift, loving the book bag she got him. It would come in handy next semester as he headed back to classes.

After Derric, Becky, and Hannah went back to San Francisco, the house seemed too quiet to Miah. Finding Maggie sipping her coffee and staring into space one morning shortly after they left, he knew she was feeling it, too. That night he suggested they all go into town after dinner to see a new movie that was out. It was a comedy, and they all laughed until they couldn't laugh any more. It was just what they needed to lighten the atmosphere.

Their church had a huge New Year's Eve party, so Maggie was busy for days preparing all the goodies she had volunteered to make for the party. Miah and Odee helped her make her famous popcorn balls, which were soft and chewy. Miah and Odee each ate two of them the night they made them!

The next day was New Year's Eve, so they loaded all the goodies into Odee's truck and headed over to the church. Janie, Carson, and their parents were all there, too, so it was lots of fun for all of them. There was food aplenty, and all kinds of games and prizes. Some of the youth group had formed a band, so there was music and dancing all night long. At midnight, as Miah gave Janie a New Year's kiss, he felt like the luckiest person in the world.

The second semester of college started right after New Year's Day, and Miah was quickly immersed in classes and chores. By the end of the month, it didn't seem like there had ever been a break! The week of his birthday, Miah got a call from Child Protective Services explaining that his mother had left a letter for him to open on his eighteenth birthday. They informed him they would include it with some papers they needed to send him to close out his file.

The day he got the packet in the mail, he sat down at the kitchen table just staring at it. Maggie had mentioned it at supper and told him he needed to open the packet and sign and send back anything necessary to close out his file. So, he sat there looking at it, wondering what was inside. Finally, Maggie came back into the kitchen with Odee and saw Miah just sitting there staring at the envelope.

"Would it help if we opened it with you," she asked Miah. When Miah nodded his head yes, she and Odee sat down at the table with him. Maggie gently pulled the packet toward her and carefully opened it. She took out the forms that needed Miah's signature and placed them in front of him. When he saw what they were, he quickly signed them and placed them back in the envelope that was included in the package. Odee suggested he take it to the post office himself to ensure it was returned. Miah just nodded. The only thing left was a sealed envelope that had Miah's name on it.

"How 'bout we give you some privacy to read the letter from your mom, okay?" Maggie suggested. Again, Miah nodded. Maggie opened the envelope carefully and placed the letter in front of Miah where he could read it easily. Then she and Odee left the room.

After a few moments of staring straight ahead, Miah finally picked up the letter and read his mother's handwriting.

Dear Miah,

I have been very sick, and I know I have passed if you are reading this letter. I want to tell you a couple of things that I couldn't tell you when I was alive, especially since you were still so young. You had a great father, Miah, whom you are named for. He was a soldier in the Army and was sent to Iraq just before you turned two. He loved you, Miah, more than life itself. I want you to know that. Unfortunately, his tour of duty kept getting extended, and we never saw him alive again. He was killed in the line of duty. After his funeral, I was given a life-long stipend that he had earned and a check with his earnings and signing bonuses. I used the stipend to help support us, but I invested the check. By the time you are eighteen, it should be well over one hundred thousand dollars. I hope it will make your life a little easier or at least help in insuring you get a college education.

I pray you can forgive me for not telling you more about your father, but talking about it was still so painful, and then I got sick and could not bring myself to tell you one more heartbreaking thing about your life. We both had to leave you before you were grown, and I could only pray that you would find a family to love you as much as we did. I hope you have a wonderful life, and learn to love and accept Christ as your Savior so we can meet again in heaven. I love you so much Miah, you are my pride and joy. It is so hard to say good-bye. Be a good person and always remember what I told you from the start: God is with you, and there is always hope. Never forget that, son; it will keep you strong and point you in the right direction. I promise you that. Know that I am always in your heart.

Forever,
Your loving mother

Miah read her last words as tears coursed down his cheeks and fell on the letter. Quickly, he snatched it up, trying to protect the last thing she had shared with him. It was such a long time ago, but Miah swore he could feel her presence as if she were sitting beside him. He sat at the table, lost in thought, until Maggie finally came back in the kitchen to see if he was okay. Sitting beside him, she simply took his hand in hers and gave him time to pull himself together.

Eventually, Miah pushed the letter over to Maggie so she could read it. When finished, she stood up, put her arms around Miah, and whispered, "We are the family she wanted you to have, son, the family that loves you just as much as she did."

Miah could only nod as he tried desperately to hold it together. Finally, giving in, he put his head on his hands and wept. He wept for his father, he wept for his mother, and he wept for all the years he was made to feel worthless. Then he wept for the incredible God who led him to his life with the Hewitts and for his heavenly Father, who knew him by name and had died to wash away the sins of the world.

Chapter 22

A couple of days later, Miah was ready to discuss the money his mother had left him. The paperwork had been sent to Child Protective Services, and they had acknowledged receipt. That chapter of his life was over. Now he had a large sum of money to decide what to do with. He told Maggie and Odee the only thing he really needed was a more dependable vehicle. They had done more than enough so far. He wanted to buy a new car with some of the money and invest the rest. He thought he could do well enough in college to qualify for the additional scholarship money, so he didn't think he would need it for that. Still, it would be there if he did.

Odee told him he thought that was smart. They would go find a car he wanted and then speak to a financial institution about reinvesting the rest of the money. Miah actually got a bit excited about looking for a vehicle, so they planned to do it that very weekend.

On Saturday, they drove to a huge auto mall and started looking at cars. Miah had done his research as usual and thought he wanted a small, dependable car that got decent gas mileage. Odee suggested a small Ford or Chevy, but Miah had seen something else he wanted to consider. He liked BMWs, but he knew they were expensive. Still, they decided to check them out. When they pulled into that particular section of the auto mall, a small, unusual car attracted Miah's attention right away in the lot next door. Pointing out the bright blue car, he asked Odee what it was. Odee told him it was a Mini Cooper, and that it got excellent gas mileage. Miah was sold from the start, so they changed directions and drove up to the dealership. Odee went in to find someone who could get them a key so they could take it for a test drive. Before the day was over,

Miah found himself the proud owner of a brand-new Mini Cooper. He saved a lot of money because it was last year's model, but it was new, dependable, and all his. The rest of the money would be reinvested and would be available for the future whenever he needed it.

That night he pulled out his Bible, looking for a particular verse. Checking the little cheat sheet he used time and time again, he looked for verses that pertained to thankfulness. There were multiple passages about thankfulness to God, but one verse stood out.

> Let us come before him with thanksgiving and extol Him with music and song. For the LORD is the great God, the great King above all Gods. (Ps. 95:2–3 NIV)

Miah thought this said exactly what he was feeling. He wished he had been mature enough in his faith to remember his prayers after his mother died. He had tried to pray at his first foster home, but the other kids made fun of him and he quickly gave it up. Now that he had accepted God into his heart, he understood that even his ignorance had not kept God away. He had been with him and guided him the whole time, leading him to the Hewitts who helped him restore what his mother had started so long ago. He had learned so much and had so much to be thankful for, and he would never be kept from prayers again. He knew without a doubt that God was there for him in good times and bad. He would never forget that, either. He bowed his head and thanked Him for all he had: his new car, the money invested for his future, and his family. His mother could rest assured that he would meet her again one day in heaven!

The rest of the second semester went quickly, and Miah was out for the summer mid-way through May. He planned to take a couple of on-line classes, but that was easy for him after all the schooling he had accomplished that way in the past. He would still have time to work at the farm and even take some time off for a day trip if he wanted. He was excited about his second year of college and already thinking about a degree in business, although the agriculture class he planned to take on-line during the summer looked very interesting, too. He still had plenty of time to make up his mind.

Graduating in June, Janie was already signed up at the community college starting in September. Unlike Miah, she knew exactly what she wanted to do. She was going to study journalism and creative writing. She had always shared Miah's passion for writing and planned to be an author one day. Nothing was going to steer her away from those goals. Miah, loving writing and reading himself, understood completely.

Miah's second year of college was just as busy as the first. It was nice having Janie around the college, even though they didn't share any classes. Miah had enjoyed his agricultural class over the summer, which led him to consider a double major going forward. He felt he could fit in a couple of extra classes until he made up his mind since he wasn't ready to let either business or agricultural studies end completely. He was maintaining a very high grade-point average in college and had already qualified for additional scholarship funds. In fact, he had a letter from the University of Ohio offering a full ride in their agricultural engineering program. He eventually decided to go with it. He wanted to stay in Ohio to be close to Janie.

There had only been one little glitch during Miah's second year at college. John, the last foster care parent Miah had run away from who had later approached him and Janie during their Christmas shopping trip, had been arrested for suspicion of abuse of another foster care child. It had been on the news, and when Miah saw the scared little boy who had come forward, he contacted Child Protective Services and told them it had happened to him as well. Miah had then been subpoenaed to appear at the court trial and testify to the abuse he had suffered at John's hands. While it had been a traumatic experience for Miah, it was finally over. At least Miah had the satisfaction of knowing the man could not hurt any more children. His foster care license had been taken away, and he would be in prison for a long, long time.

Miah's two years at the University of Ohio were tough but rewarding, and before he knew it, he was graduating with honors, of course. Once again, Derric and Becky came home for the ceremony bringing Hannah and her little brother, Hunter. They couldn't wait to see Uncle Miah, and everyone laughed when the two-and-a-half-year-old Hunter pranced around the house wearing Miah's graduation cap. Janie and her parents were there as well. They were all so proud of Miah. He felt like he was on top of the world.

After getting his agricultural engineering degree, Miah decided to take enough classes to add a business degree. Janie still had another year of college, so he would come back to the farm and do them on-line. Odee was thrilled to have him back, and even opened up a bit about some of his ideas for making a few changes. The spare bedroom was once again his home, making Maggie happy, too!

Miah felt like more than two years had passed since he had left the farm. Odee had hired a boy from church who lived nearby to come over and help with chores before and after school, but Miah could see where some things had slipped. He also thought Odee looked a lot more tired than he had two years ago. He dug in, and within a few weeks, he thought things were looking better. Odee had perked up, enjoying Miah's company and help on the farm. Even Maggie commented on the differences, praising Miah's efforts and telling him over and over that it was so good to have him back.

Once the farm was back in ship-shape condition, Miah began to talk to Odee about making a few changes and even offering to fund some of it with his own money. Although he now had the credentials to obtain a high-level job, Miah's first choice would be to run the farm, expanding it a bit to support another family. The only problem was doing it in a way that would not offend Odee, but Miah was convinced he could make it happen.

Miah's memories of his foster care years and the years on the road were fading fast now. He could hardly remember a time when he hadn't been part of the Hewitt family where he knew he was loved and appreciated. He still had an occasional thought about the terrors he had survived, but now he had the realty of family and friends to counter those thoughts. The love that surrounded him today totally outweighed his troubled past.

Janie and Miah were inseparable now and had become the best of friends. They told each other everything, and Miah had even opened up to her about his past. He knew he could count on her for support and understanding, and it was a wonderful feeling to be number one in someone's life. He couldn't imagine life without her by his side. They had already started talking about life after college, and Miah was excited to think about all the possibilities.

Chapter 23

Miah and Janie were planning a trip to the Heavenly Home for Girls. It had been almost five years since he had snuck back to the home to see the baby he had dropped off on their doorstep. He had written to the owner, Mrs. Harper, and received word that she had adopted the baby after they had petitioned for news of the mother or father without results. She was part of a large family now, and they all adored her. She had ten sisters who all lived at the Heavenly Home for Girls, which had simply become the Harper House over the years. She welcomed a visit from Miah, thanking him for the wonderful gift he had delivered to them.

Miah had talked to Maggie about asking Janie to marry him after graduation, and they had shopped secretly for just the right ring. He had also made the trip to see Janie's parents asking their permission to marry her. They gave him their blessing, welcoming Miah without hesitation. They had come to love him over the years and were proud of all he had accomplished since he came to the Hewitts. Miah could hardly wait to ask Carter to be his best man! But he had to get a yes from his girl first.

Janie didn't know it but, when they made the trip to visit the girls' home, Miah planned to surprise her by taking her to the big farmhouse that was for sale down the road from the Hewitts. His plan was to propose to her and suggest buying the home for their new future! He had plenty of money for a substantial down payment thanks to his mom and dad. He wished they were here to be part of it all, but he loved Maggie and Odee, too! He knew his parents would be proud of all of them.

After graduation, Janie had accepted a job at a local newspaper, writing a daily column. Miah seemed anxious to make plans to visit the Harper House, so they agreed on a date. She didn't really understand all of Miah's excitement about the trip, but she knew he wanted to make sure the little girl he had known as an infant was well cared for. He had felt bad for many years about leaving her on that doorstep.

They headed out on a sunny June morning, driving Miah's dependable little Mini Cooper. They were hoping to be at the Harper Home by lunchtime. Mrs. Harper planned on having them join everyone for lunch. Miah chatted the whole way there, and Janie assumed he must be very nervous about meeting the little girl. She still had no idea about his secondary plans.

When they arrived at the house where Miah had left the baby, he noticed that the "Heavenly Home for Girls" sign above the first-floor windows had been replaced by a sign that said, "Harper House." They parked in the drive and walked up to the front door. Before they could even knock, the door flew open, and a little girl peered out the door at them.

"Hello," she said. "Are you Miah?" She was about five or six with curly brown hair and bright blue eyes. Miah knew immediately this had to be Gracie.

Before Miah and Janie could answer, they heard a voice in the background asking Gracie to wait a minute before opening the door. *Too late*, thought Miah!

"Please come in," Gracie continued, as an older woman arrived at the door.

"Yes, welcome. I am Mrs. Harper," the woman replied. "We have been expecting you."

"Thank you," Miah said nervously. "This is my girlfriend, Janie."

"She's lovely," Gracie exclaimed sincerely, making Janie blush.

"Come, in, come in," Mrs. Harper said, ushering them inside. "Please come meet our girls."

"Only seven of my sisters are here today," confided Gracie importantly. "My big sisters went to see a movie that is too grown up for me. I hope you like soup and sandwiches. Miss Jackie and Miss Jeannie make the best soup and sandwiches! And we all made cupcakes for dessert. You are going to love them!" Gracie grabbed one of each of their hands leading them into the dining room where seven girls sat at a long dining room table waiting for lunch.

Mrs. Harper shook her head laughing. "Meet Gracie," she said. "She is our little social butterfly. Girls, this is Mr. Miah and Miss Janie." Going around the table, she introduced the seven girls: Lucy, Nora, Olivia, Emma, Sophie, Maddi, and Gabbi.

"And these two ladies are Miss Jeannie and Miss Jackie," Mrs. Harper added, as two ladies came in carrying a larger platter of sandwiches and a tray of soup dishes. They greeted Miah and Janie and showed them to their seats after setting the food on the table. It was no surprise to Miah when Mrs. Harper asked for a volunteer to say the prayer and Gracie raised her hand.

"I will, I will!" She exclaimed. "Let us pray."

All the girls smiled and bowed their heads as Gracie said a prayer thanking God for their food, each other, and everything she could think of including Miah and Janie. When she finished, they all said amen and praised her for the great prayer. Gracie beamed as they started passing around the sandwiches.

After a great lunch with colorful cupcakes for dessert, the girls were excited to show Miah and Janie around Harper House.

"We have made a lot of improvements," Mrs. Harper commented, "and the girls love to add their own little touches." They headed up the stairs, and Miah and Janie were enchanted when they walked into a huge room at the top. It had been divided into several smaller rooms with colorful partitions covered with hundreds of photos and names of the girls who resided in that section. There were bunkbeds and dressers along each section and small tables and chairs in the middle of each area. It looked fresh and personal, and Miah could see that the girls all loved it. They wound their way through the home, and the girls showed them a library with shelves and shelves of books, a couple of classrooms, and private quarters for Mrs. Harper. They could also see a hallway that led to the kitchen with doors they assumed led to rooms for Miss Jeanie and Miss Jackie.

"This is amazing," Janie commented. "You all have a beautiful home."

"Thank you," Mrs. Harper replied. "We have tried to make it a place where we can all thrive. The girls are getting older, so we just keep making revisions as we go along. We love it though, don't we, girls?" She looked around at all the girls who nodded in agreement.

Miah was completely sold. He was happy that the little girl he had left on the doorstep had landed in such a loving, happy environment.

"Thank you for inviting us for lunch," he said. "This house is wonderful, and I am so happy for all of you!"

"I love to read and write," Janie added. "I am so happy you have books and classrooms for learning."

"Oh, Miss Debbie, Miss Sarah, and Miss Katie teach us lessons," Gracie offered. "They are all teachers now! Well Katie is *almost* a teacher."

As Janie discussed classes and subjects with the girls, Mrs. Harper pulled Miah into her office. "I think this will be a little more private," she told Miah. "Do you have any questions for me?"

Miah told Mrs. Harper a little bit about his story and why he had dropped the baby off on her doorstep. He shared his concern over the past few years about what he had done and how it might have impacted her. The tears in his eyes told the rest of the story.

Mrs. Harper filled him in on her past as well, admitting her own shortcomings. She told him about falling in love with Grace and adopting her. She assured him that things had changed for the better once she had adopted all the girls, sharing her love for them and all they had accomplished. Miah admired her courage in admitting her past mistakes and her generosity in taking on all the girls. He was reassured he had made the right decision in leaving the baby here all those years ago. He had no doubt at all about the fact that she was loved and cared for. Miah told Mrs. Harper he would like to make a donation to the Harper House, and in spite of her protests, he gave her the check he had brought with him. He wanted to contribute to the welfare of the little baby girl who had touched his heart as an infant.

They walked back to the parlor with mutual respect for one another. Miah and Janie said their goodbyes but were surprised when, at the last minute, little Gracie ran to them hugging them both together. "Please come and see us again," she said earnestly. "We really like you!"

Miah and Janie assured her they would try to stop by another time and said their final goodbyes. They headed to the car and were both happy they had made the trip. Janie could tell Miah was relieved about the home and the little girl. She thought the home was incredible, and it was obvious that all the girls loved being there. Gracie was simply adorable, and she couldn't imagine a better place for her to grow up. She lacked for nothing and was loved by all. She would certainly encourage Miah to return and could hardly wait to see what the future held for little Gracie Harper.

Chapter 24

On their way home, Miah was a little quiet, but Janie thought he looked happy. Every now and then, she caught him smiling. Janie chatted about her job and confided in Miah that what she really wanted to do some day was write a novel. He smiled at her affectionately, telling her he couldn't wait to read it. Janie fell in love with him all over again!

After hours of driving, they were finally nearing home. It was almost dusk when Miah pulled into a driveway down the road from the Hewitts. He got out of the car and motioned to Janie to do the same. She climbed out of the car with a puzzled look on her face.

"What do you think about this place?" he asked Janie. She walked up the driveway with him where she saw a big, sprawling farmhouse with a For Sale sign in the yard. It was weathered and needed some work, but, like Miah, Janie could see the possibilities. She smiled as she pictured a new coat of paint, curtains at the windows, and flowers everywhere. She could imagine apples on the apple trees off to the side of the property and freshly mown grass.

Miah saw the expression on Janie's face and new she was thinking about how it would look once they fixed it up. It was all he needed to take the next step. Kneeling in the grass right beside the For Sale sign, he reached in his pocket and pulled out the ring box he had felt there all day long. Janie's hands flew to her mouth as she realized what was happening.

"Janie Amelia Johnson," he started, "will you do me the honor of becoming my wife?"

Janie was speechless as she gazed at the beautiful ring Miah held out toward her. She was already crying tears of happiness when she threw her arms around him and said, "Yes! Of course, I will be your wife. I love you beyond words!"

They were both laughing and crying as Miah slipped the ring on her finger. She marveled at how well it fit, and Miah admitted he had gotten her ring size from her parents when he asked them for permission to marry her. He felt like today was the happiest day of his life! He told Janie, if she approved, he wanted to buy the house and start fixing it up while they made plans to be married. He was hoping to continue to help Odee run the farm and enlarge it a bit to support them as well. Living here would make it easy to go back and forth. Janie thought it was a wonderful idea. They walked all around the property, holding hands and talking about their plans for the future.

As they got in the car to finish the trip home and share their news, he beamed at the young lady sitting next to him. She had been at camp when he accepted Christ into his heart and when he had to face John on the shopping trip. He had shared his past with her and his dreams of the future. Holding her hand as she glanced at the engagement ring he had placed on her finger, he thought they were a perfect match! Little did he know, she was thinking the exact same thing!

Miah and Janie were quiet as they made their way back to the Hewitt farm where both of their families were waiting to hear the good news. Deep in his own thoughts, Miah realized that for the first time in a long time, he felt like he had truly found his place in life. He silently gave thanks to God promising himself to share more time with Him later and knowing that God's blessing on his marriage was of utmost importance. He already had the blessings of both of their families and felt confident about the coming meeting. As he pulled into the driveway at the farm, he felt a little tickle on the back of his neck and he was pretty sure his mom was giving him her blessing as well!

Epilogue

He tucked the blanket around the old man's legs in the wheelchair as they made their way to inspect the barn and milking shed. Miah knew he wouldn't be happy until he had seen it all. Glancing over his shoulder, he winked at the teenage girl who was fussing over Maggie as she sat in a rocking chair on the porch watching everything. He knew Hannah would make sure her grandmother had everything she needed. His seven-year-old twin boys circled Odee's wheelchair shouting the whole time about the new baby calf. Odee and Miah both smiled, remembering another time when a young boy had watched his first calf being born.

Miah had graduated with honors years ago and was now running the farm, having obtained degrees in *both* business and agriculture. He and Janie had been married for almost ten years now, and Janie had gone on to get her degree in journalism and was happily working on her third novel. Elliott and Elijah, the twins, loved everything about the farm and already helped with most of the chores. Their sister, Lilly (named after his mother), was probably up in the loft at this very moment playing with the new kittens that had been born recently. Miah knew it was going to be hard for her to let them go when the time came.

They all still attended the same church the Hewitts had taken him to when he first arrived that cold, January day at their doorstep. Derric and Becky had moved back to Ohio, living in a beautiful house on a lake and making it easier to spend more time at the farm with the family. Becky taught school in town, and Derric consulted with a huge computer firm, traveling often, but working the rest of the time from home. It was hard to believe they had two teenagers now. *How time flies*, Miah thought to himself.

He and Janie bought the house next door to the Hewitts when they married, remodeling it completely over the years and making it very convenient for Miah to come over and run the farm just as they had planned. The farm had been expanded over the years as well with an up-to-date milking shed that was triple the original size and the addition of more than a dozen new cows. The barn had been rebuilt recently, too, and now had enough room for twenty cows. The crops had been expanded to include hay and straw in addition to the corn needed to feed the cows. Miah's agricultural degree had come in handy, giving him the knowledge required to plant and harvest more crops and utilize more of the land. With Derric's assistance, Odee's original spreadsheets had been improved and expanded, utilizing new accounting and inventory programs Derric had written, and Miah had implemented. The brothers had become fast friends, consulting with Odee and working together to improve an already profitable enterprise. The Hewitt Farm flourished as did everyone involved with it.

They had hired a housekeeper/caregiver to live with Maggie and Odee recently because they needed a little extra attention and could no longer handle the day-to-day upkeep, even though they tried. Odee had suffered a stroke a couple of years ago and had recently had a knee replaced. Maggie was a bit hard of hearing and tired out easily, but otherwise the Hewitts were still doing pretty well. Miah could not bear to think of losing them yet. He was so proud to carry on the legacy Odee had started and determined to make it even better.

Miah half-listened to Odee as he explained milking to the twins who listened raptly to Odee's every word. He understood their adoration of their grandfather, remembering how much he had wanted a grandfather at their age. His thoughts then shifted to his own mother and how hard she had worked to make sure Miah knew he was loved. She had invested in Miah's future wisely without ever saying a word. The money had grown over the years, but it wasn't the money that Miah was most thankful for. It was the connection to God she had instilled in him at a very young age. He had lost it briefly, but God had led him to this wonderful family where it had been reborn.

He shared that with his own children now, helping them to know God was there in both happy and troubled times. He used the same words with them his mom had used with him, knowing they would understand in their own time just as he had. He knew God was right there with them always, and that his mom was up there in heaven, happy he had found such a wonderful family with whom to share his life. When he prayed with his children at night, it was her words that ended their prayers: "God is with us, and there is always hope." Amen!

From the Author

T hank you for reading this story. I hope you enjoyed reading it as much as I enjoyed writing it! I welcome your comments and suggestions for future books, so please share them at www.jclafler.com or e-mail me at jclafler@hotmail.com. God bless!

Other Books by J. C. Lafler

Lost and Found: A story of faith, love and survival

A young boy who finds himself in a big city with no memory of the past and no one to help him, must find a way to survive searching for food and water in some of the city's worst areas. As flashbacks and questions about the past begin to overwhelm him, he leans on the sanctuary of a church and the help of strangers to see him through. *Lost and Found* is one boy's story of finding his way back to faith, hope, and love.

Reader's review: "What an imaginative and beautifully written story. I was totally caught up by the beginning poem and then engrossed as the story unfolded. I loved the way the boy began to feel the love surrounding him . . . slowly, as the petals of a flower opening . . . and then came to the realization that God was actually watching over and loving him via the special 'angels' he encountered. The epilogue was such a satisfying surprise! You did a delightful job of sharing God's love for everyone and how He has us in His hands no matter where life leads."

Amazing Grace: A story about the life-changing power of faith and forgiveness

As a group of young girls find themselves in an unloving environment, eleven-year-old Sarah uses her childhood Bible, the only thing she has left of her parents, to teach the other girls about faith and help them cope with their situation. A baby left on their doorstep adds strain to an already difficult situation but draws the girls together and brings love and understanding into their lives. A tragic turn of events uncovers a chance for learning about forgiveness and finding love and happiness.

Reader's review: "*Amazing Grace* is the second novel by J. C. Lafler, and once again, she has pulled us into a heart-warming story that will have you quickly turning the pages to find out what will happen next. This author has a way of making you feel the emotions of her characters, and it is just what my heart needed. I am looking forward to her next novel."

Order Information

To order additional copies of this book, please visit
www.redemption-press.com.
Also available on Amazon.com and BarnesandNoble.com
Or by calling toll free 1-844-2REDEEM.